There was silence for such a long time Kennedy wondered if there was a problem with Carl's antique cell phone. Finally, Rose asked, "And so what happens if you get pregnant, and you're too young to actually have a baby?"

Defying all laws of inertia, the acceleration of Kennedy's heart rate crashed to a halt like a car plowing into a brick wall. "What do you mean?"

"Like, what if you're too young but you still get pregnant?"

"How young?" Kennedy spoke both words clearly and slowly, as if rushing might drive the timid voice away for good.

"Like thirteen."

Praise for *Unplanned*
by Alana Terry

"Deals with **one of the most difficult situations a pregnancy center could ever face**. The message is **powerful** and the story-telling **compelling**." ~ William Donovan, *Executive Director Anchorage Community Pregnancy Center*

"Alana Terry does an amazing job tackling a very **sensitive subject from the mother's perspective**." ~ Pamela McDonald, *Director Okanogan CareNet Pregnancy Center*

"**Thought-provoking** and intense ... Shows **different sides of the abortion argument**." ~ Sharee Stover, *Wordy Nerdy*

"Alana has a way of sharing the gospel **without being preachy**." ~ Phyllis Sather, *Purposeful Planning*

She wouldn't be victimized again. She had to get away. She wouldn't let him catch up to her. A footstep on the concrete. Not a fabrication. Not this time. It was real. Real as the scientific method. Real as her parents' love for her. Real as death. In the pitch darkness, she rushed ahead, running her fingers along the grimy wall so she would know which way to go as she sprinted down the walkway. What did contracting a few germs compare to getting murdered?

How close was he now? And why couldn't she have remembered her pepper spray? She strained her ears but only heard the slap of her boots on the walkway, the sound of her own panting, the pounding of her heart valves in her pericardial sac. She didn't want to stop, couldn't slow down, but she had to save her strength. She needed energy to fight back when he caught up. She couldn't hear him, but that didn't mean he wasn't coming.

Any second now.

Praise for *Paralyzed*
by Alana Terry

"Alana Terry has **done the almost unthinkable**; she has written a story with **raw emotions of real people**, not the usual glossy Christian image." ~ Jasmine Augustine, Tell Tale Book Reviews

"Alana has a way of **using fiction to open difficult issues** and make you think." ~ Phyllis Sather, Author of *Purposeful Planning*

"Once again, Ms. Terry brings a **sensitive but important issue to the forefront** without giving an answer. She **leaves it up to the reader** to think about and decide." ~ Darla Meyer, Book Reviewer

Without warning, the officer punched Reuben in the gut. Reuben doubled over as the cop brought his knee up to his face. Reuben staggered.

"You dirty n—." Without warning, the cop whipped out his pistol and smashed its butt against Reuben's head. He crumpled to the ground, where the officer's boots were ready to meet him with several well-placed kicks.

Throwing all rational thoughts aside, Kennedy jumped on his back. Anything to get him to stop beating Reuben. The officer swore and swatted at her. Kennedy heard herself screaming but had no idea what she was saying. She couldn't see anything else, nor could she understand how it was that when her normal vision returned, she was lying on her back, but the officer and Reuben were nowhere to be seen.

Praise for *Policed*
by Alana Terry

"*Policed* could be taken **from the headlines of today's news**." ~ Meagan Myhren-Bennett, *Blooming with Books*

"**A provocative story** with authentic characters." ~ Sheila McIntyre, *Book Reviewer*

"It is important for Christian novelists to address today's issues like police misconduct and racism. Too often writers tiptoe around **serious issues faced by society**." ~ Wesley Harris, *Law Enforcement Veteran*

"Focuses on a prevalent issue in today's society. Alana **pushes the boundaries more than any other Christian writer**." ~ Angie Stormer, *Readaholic Zone*

Wayne Abernathy, the Massachusetts state senator, was towering over a teenage boy who sat crumpled over the Lindgrens' dining room table.

"I don't care what you have to do to fix him," Wayne blasted at Carl.

Kennedy froze. Nobody heard her enter. Carl sat with his back to her, but she could still read the exhaustion in his posture.

Wayne brought his finger inches from the boy's nose. "Do whatever you have to do, Pastor. Either straighten him up, or so help me, he's got to find some other place to live."

Kennedy bit her lip, trying to decide if it would be more awkward to leave, make her presence known, or stay absolutely still.

Wayne's forehead beaded with sweat, and his voice quivered with conviction. "It's impossible for any son of mine to turn out gay."

Praise for *Straightened*
by Alana Terry

"Alana doesn't take a side, but she makes you really think. She **presents both sides of the argument in a very well written way**." ~ Diane Higgins, *The Book Club Network*

"No matter what conviction you have on the subject, I'm fairly certain **you will find that this novel has a character who accurately represents that viewpoint**." ~ Justin, Avid Reader

"Alana Terry doesn't beat up her readers, but, rather she gets them to either examine their own beliefs or encourages them to **find out for themselves what they believe and what the Bible says**." ~ Jasmine Augustine, *Tell Tale Book Reviews*

She shook her head. "I don't know. I can't say. I just know that something is wrong here. It's not safe." She clenched his arm with white knuckles. "Please, I can't ... We have to ..." She bit her lip.

He frowned and let out a heavy sigh. "You're absolutely certain?"

She nodded faintly. "I think so."

"It's probably just nerves. It's been a hard week for all of us." There was a hopefulness in his voice but resignation in his eyes.

She sucked in her breath. "This is different. Please." She drew her son closer to her and lowered her voice. "For the children."

"All right." He unbuckled his seatbelt and signaled one of the flight attendants. "I'm so sorry to cause a problem," he told her when she arrived in the aisle, "but you need to get my family off this plane. Immediately."

Praise for *Turbulence*
by Alana Terry

"This book is **hard to put down** and is a **suspenseful roller coaster of twists and turns**." ~ Karen Brooks, *The Book Club Network*

"I've enjoyed all of the Kennedy Stern novels so far, but **this one got to me in a more personal way** than the others have." ~ *Fiction Aficionado*

"I love that the author is **not afraid to deal with tough issues all believers deal with**." ~ Kit Hackett, *YWAM Missionary*

To my very own "Grandma Lucy," a missionary, Bible smuggler, prayer warrior, and encourager. I can't wait to see you again in heaven. I love you so much.

1926-2016

Note: The views of the characters in this novel do not necessarily reflect the views of the author.

The characters in this book are fictional. Any resemblance to real persons is coincidental. No part of this book may be reproduced in any form (electronic, audio, print, film, etc.) without the author's written consent.

www.alanaterry.com

Turbulence

a novel by Alana Terry

"Keep me as the apple of your eye;
hide me in the shadow of your wings."
Psalm 17:8

CHAPTER 1

T minus 3 hours 57 minutes

"Thanks for the ride." Kennedy gave Dominic an awkward smile.

He stepped forward. It would be the perfect time for a hug, but she knew better than to expect something like that. He cleared his throat. "Merry Christmas." He glanced at Kennedy's roommate Willow, who ran her fingers through her dyed hair. "Nice to meet you," he said.

"Yup. Thanks." Willow picked up her two bags without looking back and walked into Logan Airport.

Kennedy hesitated before turning away. "I better go." She shuffled from one foot to another, hating herself for feeling as foolish as a seventh-grader at her first boy-girl dance. She glanced up.

Dominic smiled again. Over the past semester, she and the police chaplain had gone out for coffee twice, dinner once, and a picnic lunch on Boston Common, but they never

1

used words like *dating* or *girlfriend*. Everything about Dominic was slow. Peaceful. Sometimes Kennedy wished she could be as relaxed as he was. Other times, she was certain the deceleration would drive her insane.

"Well, have a great Christmas." He shut the trunk, and with his car effectively shielding them from any hint of physical contact, he gave one last wave. "Enjoy Alaska."

Her roommate was already halfway to the electronic check-ins before Kennedy could catch up. Willow adjusted her braided fabric carry-on over her shoulder. "Say good-bye to lover boy?"

Kennedy unbuttoned her leather coat. "I'm kind of hungry. Let's find our gate and then grab something to eat."

Willow typed into her cell while she walked. "Whatever." Her phone played a short electric guitar run. She stared at her incoming text. "Oh, my dad's wondering if you're a carnivore or not."

Kennedy didn't know how to answer. She'd never met Willow's parents before, and as excited as she was for the chance to spend Christmas break with her roommate's family in rural Alaska, she wasn't sure how well she'd fit in. "How do the rest of your family eat?"

Willow scrolled down on her screen. "Dad's a carnivore. Mom's like me, basically vegan except we'll have dairy if it's from our herd. You can choose. Meat or not?"

Kennedy shrugged. "Sure. I guess."

"All right. He'll be glad to hear that."

They were halfway to their terminal when the Guns N' Roses riff sounded again. Willow stared at her screen. "Ok, now he's asking how you feel about moose."

Growing up, Kennedy had never paid much attention to the kind of protein on her plate. *Meat* meant any animal that wasn't poultry or fish, but she was pretty sure moose had never made it on her palate before.

"I guess that's fine."

Willow wrinkled her nose. "I should warn you, it's probably roadkill."

Kennedy wasn't sure she'd heard correctly. "Road what?"

"Roadkill. You know. Driver hits a moose, moose bites it, and nobody wants to waste that much meat." She pouted at Kennedy's raised eyebrows. "You've got a lot to learn about Alaska."

Even though Willow was still typing into her phone, Kennedy had to hurry to keep up. "Maybe it's best I don't know where it's coming from."

Willow shrugged, but Kennedy thought she detected a smile hidden under her roommate's rather bored expression.

So far, she and Willow had enjoyed their second year together as Harvard roommates. Kennedy had gone into her sophomore year so terrified of falling behind that she actually ended up ahead. She'd finished her final paper for her Shakespeare class the week before Thanksgiving and handed in her fruit fly lab report to her biology professor a few days later. That freed up the last few weeks for her to spend extra time with Willow, who was never busy with anything unless it was memorizing lines for a play or attending theater rehearsals. The two of them had gone to the movies twice and even grabbed tickets to watch *Mama Mia* at the Boston Opera House as a fun way to kick off the Christmas season.

Or *holiday season*, as Willow and nearly everyone else on campus insisted on calling it.

The two girls found their gate and decided to kill time at a small coffee shop around the corner.

"Wait 'til you try Kaladi Brothers," Willow told her. "It makes all the coffee from the Lower 48 taste like melted snow."

Kennedy crinkled her nose at the comparison and breathed in the frothy steam wafting from her hot chocolate. She warmed her hands on the red and white cup, relishing the heat that coursed up her veins to her core, remembering

4

how anxious she'd started out this semester. How terrified she'd been at the prospect of taking two lab classes at once. As it turned out, organic chemistry wasn't nearly the nightmare she'd come to expect. Sure, it was a lot of memorization, but you'd do all right as long as you didn't fall behind.

And if there was anything Kennedy learned at Harvard so far, it was how to stay on top of her work, no matter what was going on around her. Kidnappings, panic attacks, race riots, murder investigations — she had survived them all. And now she was about to embark on a brand new adventure in Alaska, land of ice and moose and glaciers. Willow had told her they might even get to see the aurora borealis. Kennedy had never witnessed the northern lights before and hoped they'd come out at least once on her trip.

While Willow texted, Kennedy stared around at all the people, the hustle and bustle of the crowded Logan terminal. So many people going home, visiting family, reuniting with loved ones. Last year, she'd spent Christmas break getting chased by a murderous stalker. Not the most festive way to get into the holiday spirit.

Now, her heart was as cheerful as Scrooge's magnanimous nephew Fred. She'd made it through another semester with only one or two minor panic attacks on her record. She had every reason to expect a good report card, with all As except for a possible B-plus in organic chem lab. She'd worked hard, and now she was on her way to Alaska, which felt even more foreign than far-east China where her parents lived as missionaries.

The hot chocolate nearly burned her tongue as she took another sip.

She deserved this vacation. And she was going to enjoy every single moment of it.

CHAPTER 2

T minus 2 hours 39 minutes

Kennedy and Willow boarded the plane and found their seats in the very back row. As much as Kennedy hated the exhaustion and paranoia that came from flying in a pressurized cabin with hundreds of other germ-ridden strangers, she found planes to be some of the best places to people-watch. It was a good thing too, since for the next twelve hours, there wouldn't be much for her to do except read, sleep, and stare at her fellow travelers.

Her pastor's wife had given her a few books to take on her trip, missionary biographies Sandy thought she might enjoy. The Lindgrens were in the middle of a huge home remodel to give their adopted son more space and repair damages from a house fire last fall. Sandy was donating most of their books to the St. Margaret's library or else passing them on to others, which was how Kennedy ended up with a backpack full of biographies about people like Hudson

Taylor and Amy Carmichael, pioneers in the modern missions movement. She doubted it was reading her agnostic roommate would approve of, but Willow was currently obsessed with some high-def shooter game on her smartphone, so Kennedy didn't think she'd care. Besides, Willow had spent twenty minutes flirting with a math teacher from Washington at the gate and was hoping to angle her way closer to him for at least some of the flight.

Kennedy was in the aisle, which gave her a clear view of the passengers as they boarded: A short, white-haired woman with spectacles that made her look like she should be in a tree baking cookies with the Keebler elves. Ray, the twenty-something teacher who flung a charming albeit somewhat awkward grin Willow's way when he spotted her on the plane. A fat, middle-aged man in an orange Hawaiian shirt gripping the arm of a sullen-looking teenager. Her shorts might have been appropriate on a sunny beach but certainly not in the chill of Boston in December, and her Bon Jovi T-shirt was so faded it might have been as old as the band itself.

Many of the travelers appeared to be flying solo, a miscellaneous group ranging from single men in flannels and jeans all the way up to business women in heels, hose, and mercilessly pressed skirt suits. A balding man in Carhartt pants sat across from a younger one with an SVSU sweatshirt. Kennedy tried to figure out what the initials stood for.

Interspersed amongst the single travelers were a few families. A couple with four kids, none of them older than Kennedy had been when her family first moved to China, made their way toward the back of the cabin.

"I wonder if they know what century we're in," Willow muttered, raising her eyebrow at the mom's head scarf and the long denim skirts the girls wore.

Kennedy tried not to stare. They certainly weren't the type of family she was used to seeing around Cambridge. The mother sat across from Kennedy with two preschool-aged kids, a boy and girl, while the older daughters sat in the row ahead with their father, whose jet black beard reached to his chest.

"I didn't think the Amish were allowed to fly," Willow mumbled.

Kennedy couldn't tell if her roommate was joking or not. All the information she knew about the Amish came from her mom's love affair with historical romance, a genre Kennedy avoided as a rule whenever possible. Once a month or so back home, she had to sit with her mom and watch a sappy historical movie, usually about swooning heroines and sensitive heroes that more often than not made Kennedy want to barf. Some of the films were set in Amish communities. Others were on homesteads in the 1800s. It was hard for Kennedy to keep them separate in her mind.

"Actually, they're probably Mennonite," Willow finally decided. "Oh, well. At least the kids won't be too bratty and scream the whole flight. *Spare the rod,* all that junk."

Kennedy pried her eyes away to give the family a small semblance of privacy. She wondered if the children were self-conscious looking so different than everyone else. Did they care? Or were they so used to things being the way they were it didn't matter?

A rustic-looking passenger in a Seattle Seahawks hoodie plopped into the row directly in front of Willow and Kennedy. The girls wrinkled their noses at each other at the overwhelming stink of body odor and cigarettes. Willow reached into the braided bag under her seat and pulled out two air purifier necklaces she'd purchased for their flight. She handed one to Kennedy, and they both slipped the small gadgets over their heads. If there was one thing Kennedy and Willow shared, it was their desire to breathe germless, stench-free air.

Kennedy unzipped her backpack. She was in the middle of a biography about Gladys Aylward, a London parlor maid who ended up traveling to China as a missionary. When war broke out with Japan, she led over a hundred orphan children to safety. The story was mesmerizing, exciting enough to turn into a major Blockbuster success. It would sure beat those farm romances her mom watched. Kennedy only had five or six chapters left. She could probably finish it by takeoff if she jumped right in, but she waited, relishing the fact that she had absolutely no reason to rush. The plane would touch down in Detroit in two and a half hours, let off a few passengers, take a few others on, and then it was a ten-hour ride to Anchorage. Besides calling her parents when she landed, she had absolutely nothing on her to-do list. She could read during the entire flight if she wanted to, or sleep, or try to figure out Willow's silly shooter game in two-player mode. For the first time in four months, she had no lab write-ups, no research papers, no book assignments, nothing at all to worry about. She'd even promised herself not to jump ahead for her literature classes next semester. The only classic she had with her was *A Christmas Carol*, which hardly counted since she read it every December anyway. This break was all about relaxing. She still didn't know what to expect from Willow's family way out in rural Alaska, but she was ready for an adventure — an adventure she couldn't enjoy if she burdened herself with tons of assignments and self-imposed deadlines.

The seats filled up as quickly as could be expected with a hundred or more passengers with bulky luggage and winter coats banging into the seatbacks and each other. Kennedy took in a deep breath, thankful for Willow's air purifier, which looked like some kind of strange techno-amulet. Even if the benefits were all placebos, she was happy for something to give her a small edge against the germs blowing rampant around the cabin.

The two older Mennonite children carried small backpacks, and as if on some unspoken cue, they each took out a book in nearly perfect unison. Kennedy watched with curiosity. She didn't have any siblings, never knew what it was like to share a room or share her toys, what it was like to have someone to play with or pester as the mood struck. She hadn't considered herself lonely as a child, but at times like these she felt a certain heaviness in her chest as she wondered what life might have been like if her parents had decided to have more than one kid.

A row behind the older children, the mother began to read a Dr. Seuss book to the two youngest kids. Kennedy had a hard time pinpointing why she found that so strange. Was she so accustomed to picturing women in denim skirts and headscarves as strict and stoic that it was odd to think of them picking something as frivolous as *Horton Hatches an Egg*?

The mother laughed, a clear, joyful sound that forced Kennedy to study her face more closely. She was young, much younger than Kennedy had guessed when the family boarded the plane. Clear skin, shining blue eyes. Kennedy couldn't help but thinking of Scrooge's niece in *A Christmas Carol* with her little dimpled smile that Dickens lauded so eloquently.

A minute later, the wife frowned and stopped reading. What was wrong? Her daughter tugged on her sleeve, and she absently handed the girl the book before she adjusted her head covering and shifted in her seat. She stared at her two children, as if she were about to speak. She reached her hand out until she nearly brushed her husband's arm but withdrew it a second later.

Kennedy followed her gaze to the front of the plane, at two men with turbans and long beards who were boarding together. One was significantly older, but they both wore loose-fitting pants with long cotton robes instead of an American-style shirt. The noise in the cabin diminished, as two dozen whispered conversations stopped at once. Kennedy glanced around, trying to guess what was wrong. The Mennonite mother clenched her husband's shoulder. Willow must have noticed it, too. She nudged Kennedy.

"You'd think with those long beards they'd be instant

friends, wouldn't you?" Mischief danced in her eyes.

The husband turned to look at his wife. Kennedy couldn't hear their words, but the worry on both their faces was unmistakable. Meanwhile, the younger man with the turban nearly dropped a heavy briefcase he tried to heft into the overhead compartment.

"Oh, great," mumbled the Seahawks fan in front of Kennedy. "Stinking Arabs." He looked around as if trying to find a sympathetic ear. "Why they gotta put them so close to the cockpit?"

Willow smacked him on the back of his head. He turned around with an expletive, which she answered with a mini lecture about the myriad pitfalls and injustices of racial profiling. Kennedy wasn't paying attention. She was still watching the Mennonite couple, studying the way the color had all but drained from the wife's face.

"I can't say what it is," she told her husband. "I just have this feeling something is about to go wrong."

He looked at the newly boarded passengers. "Because of them?"

She shook her head. "I don't know. I can't say. I just know that something is wrong here. It's not safe." She clenched his arm with white knuckles. "Please, I can't … We have to …" She bit her lip.

The husband frowned and let out a heavy sigh. "You're absolutely certain?"

She nodded faintly. "I think so."

"It's probably just nerves. It's been a hard week for all of us." There was a hopefulness in his voice but resignation in his eyes.

She sucked in her breath. "This is different. Please." She drew her son closer to her and lowered her voice. "For the children."

"All right." He unbuckled his seatbelt and signaled one of the flight attendants. "I'm so sorry to cause a problem," he told her when she arrived in the aisle, "but you need to get my family off this plane. Immediately."

CHAPTER 3

T minus 2 hours 12 minutes

Kennedy watched while the flight attendant escorted the family down the aisle toward the exit. She had never seen anything like that happen before and couldn't stop an uneasy feeling from sloshing around in her gut, the same foreboding Scrooge must have experienced at the London Stock Exchange when he listened to the businessmen joke about their colleague's lonesome death. She was glad her roommate was giving BO Dude an Academy Award-worthy lecture against racism, or else Willow probably would have shoved her sermon down Kennedy's throat instead.

Getting a family of six off the plane took a quarter of an hour at least before the captain made his first address to the passengers. It was the typical stuff Kennedy had learned to tune out after a decade of international travel, but he included a brief comment about the Mennonites.

"Of course, safety is our first priority on this flight. We had a family choose to deboard the plane a few minutes ago, and I'd like to thank our flight attendant Tracy in the back for making that transition as smooth as possible. I want you to know we have a commitment to each passenger's personal well-being, and if there's anything we can do to make your time with us more comfortable, please don't hesitate to ask your nearest flight attendant."

After that, it was more of the usual drivel about seat trays, floatation devices, and oxygen masks.

Willow leaned back in her seat with a huff. "Some people are stubborn jerks."

"Didn't go too well?" Kennedy wondered why Willow wasted her breath on the smelly Seahawks fan but didn't bother saying so.

"I just don't get it. Are we still living in the fifties or something?" Willow crossed her arms. "I assumed the human race would have evolved a little bit farther by now." She rolled her eyes. "Can't even get on an airplane wearing foreign clothes without having racist bigots assume you're a terrorist."

Kennedy didn't know what to say. Chances were the two men in turbans were polite, respectable travelers who passed the same security screens as everyone else. But wasn't there the slightest possibility … She thought about how loosely their clothes fit. How many bombs or bomb pieces would fit strapped beneath …

No, now she was the one racial profiling. There were ample security measures, the TSA, the no-fly list, enough safeguards in place that innocent citizens could travel in peace and safety.

Right?

Kennedy tried to recall the details from a news article her dad had sent her earlier that semester. Eleven men from Jordan boarded a plane and freaked the other passengers out by their bizarre behavior, passing items in bags throughout the flight, congregating in the aisles, spending five or ten minutes at a time in the bathroom one right after another. The journalist who broke the story, a woman who had been on board and witnessed the suspicious behavior firsthand, discovered that airlines were fined if they held more than two passengers of Middle Eastern decent for extra questioning on any particular flight. Even if the men had raised security flags in the pre-boarding process, the airlines couldn't have taken any extra precautions against a group that large. There were folks who believed that what the journalist encountered was a dry run, a dress-rehearsal of sorts for putting together a bomb mid-flight, while some postulated that the men planned to take over the plane but experienced some kind of glitch in the air. Of course, others claimed the journalist was a paranoid, racist bigot who needed to shut her mouth instead of accusing innocent, peaceful travelers on unsubstantiated and somewhat vague grounds.

Kennedy knew plenty of Muslim students from Harvard, knew they weren't the crazed extremists the media made them out to be. She would be incensed on their behalf if they were made to endure an onslaught of extra or humiliating security measures simply because of their race or religion. But common courtesy and political correctness had to end somewhere, didn't they? At least when it came to protecting an airplane full of innocent civilians. Or was that the kind of reasoning that allowed cops like the one that abused her and her best friend last year to keep on wreaking their own kind of havoc on justice?

"Bunch of bigots," Willow muttered, "holding up a full flight because a few of the passengers were born in the Middle East."

Kennedy opened up her Gladys Aylward book. Maybe Willow was right. Maybe the Mennonites were racist jerks, xenophobic Americans scared of any traveler who looked even remotely different.

But Willow hadn't heard their entire conversation,

either. Hadn't heard the fear in the woman's voice. Not hatred. Not prejudice. Actual terror for her family's safety. Had the family done the right thing? Mennonites were supposedly a fairly religious group, right? Did the woman have that gift of discernment Christians sometimes talked about, that ability to hear the Holy Spirit's warnings more acutely than the average believer? If God told the woman the flight wasn't safe, did that mean Kennedy and Willow were about to head into trouble? But if that was the case, why wouldn't God have warned her, too? It didn't seem fair.

Then again, if God told Kennedy to get off the plane, if the Holy Spirit impressed on her soul that she needed to leave, would she? And risk Willow thinking she was a xenophobic racist bigot?

Or would she fasten her seatbelt, sit tight, and try to convince herself everything would be fine?

Everything would be fine, wouldn't it? Kennedy stared at the pages of her book, remembering the way God had protected Gladys Aylward and the orphans under her care so many years ago. He would take care of Kennedy that way, too.

Wouldn't he?

CHAPTER 4

T minus 1 hour 43 minutes

"Gladys Aylward? What a remarkable woman."

Kennedy was startled by the interruption to her reading.

A white-haired woman with thin-rimmed spectacles and a blouse that might have been ordered from a 1970s Sears catalog smiled at her. "I'm sorry, the restroom up front was occupied, so I came back here and couldn't help but notice your book. Are you enjoying the story?"

Kennedy didn't feel up to chatting, but since the back lavatory was occupied as well, she didn't think she had much choice. "Yeah. It's pretty interesting."

"They made a movie about her life. Did you know that?"

Kennedy shook her head.

"Well, it's quite an old one. The actress who starred in it — oh, I wish I could remember her name just now, but that's what happens when your brain gets as old as mine. Anyway, the story goes this woman became a Christian after playing the role. I assume then that you're a born-again believer?"

That phrase always struck Kennedy as strange. A *born-again believer*, as if there were any other kind. "Yeah. I am." No use getting into a theological debate on an airplane with an eighty-year-old grandmother.

A flight attendant tapped the woman on the shoulder. "Excuse me, can I squeeze past you, please?"

The old lady sat down in the Mennonite mother's empty spot and glanced at the bathroom. "Looks like I might be here a while." She smiled warmly. "My name is Lucy Jean, but I insist on being called Grandma Lucy."

"I'm Kennedy," she replied automatically, wondering how long the bathroom occupant would take.

"Kennedy. What a lovely name. You know, I still wish my parents had come up with something more creative than Lucy Jean. You don't get much plainer than that."

Kennedy was about to protest that it was an attractive name when Grandma Lucy asked, "Are you going to Detroit today?"

"No, I'm on my way to Seattle and then Anchorage to spend Christmas with my friend's family."

"How lovely. I have a granddaughter in Alaska."

"Is that where you're going?" Kennedy asked.

"No, I'm getting off in Seattle. Going home to Washington. I was just in Boston to see off my grandson. He's on his way to ..." She stopped herself to finger Kennedy's necklace from across the aisle. "What in the world is this? It looks New Age."

All Kennedy wanted to do was get back to her reading, but she gave her best impression of a smile. "It's an air purifier. You wear it around your neck, and it filters out germs and dust. My roommate got them for us for the flight." She nodded toward Willow, who was watching some violent movie on her portable screen.

Grandma Lucy frowned at the gruesome image. "And your roommate?" she asked. "Is she born-again, too?"

Kennedy was spared the chore of stammering an awkward reply when the math teacher Willow had been flirting with came up to their row.

"Bathroom full?" he asked.

Willow plucked out her earbuds and offered her most winsome grin. "Hey, Ray. I was hoping we'd bump into each other during the flight."

Kennedy unbuckled her safety belt. "It looks like there's a line, so why don't you take my seat and I'll come over here." She stepped across the aisle and sat in the window seat beside Grandma Lucy. Her contacts were getting dry anyway, so now was probably as good a time as any to take a break from reading.

Grandma Lucy took Kennedy's hand in hers. Her skin was surprisingly soft for someone with so many wrinkles. "That was sweet of you, dear. Now let me take a look at you." She stared for several seconds before she gave her hand a squeeze. "You don't have to tell me. Let me guess. You're studying to be a missionary, aren't you?"

Kennedy slipped her hand away, surprised at how warm it felt. "A doctor, actually."

Grandma Lucy nodded, as if she had known that all along. "Medical missions, then?"

Kennedy didn't know what to say. Did Grandma Lucy's version of a *born-again believer* require some sort of ministry focus to prove your devotion?

"I'm not sure. I'm still doing my undergrad studies, so I guess I have plenty of time to figure that out." She let out an uncomfortable laugh.

Grandma Lucy chuckled too, tentatively as if she weren't sure what was so funny. "It's just that when I first looked at you, something in my spirit said *missionary*. I'm sure that's what I heard." She frowned and looked around her, as if her train of thought had derailed and she had to visibly track it down.

Kennedy had an unsettled feeling in the base of her spine. Why did it seem as though every other Christian on this flight was getting direct messages from the Lord except for her? Had God ever spoken to her that way before? Or maybe he had tried, and Kennedy just didn't know what to listen for.

"You're sure you're not a missionary?" Grandma Lucy pressed.

"No, but my parents are."

Grandma Lucy's face lit up before Kennedy could continue. "That's what it was. I knew you had a missions call on your life the moment I saw you with that book. My family was good friends with Gladys, you know. She came to visit us on more than one occasion when we lived in Shanghai."

"Really?" Kennedy's interest was piqued, and since Willow was busy laughing with her new travel partner, Kennedy figured she may as well try to enjoy her conversation.

"My parents were missionaries in China. I was born over there, in fact, and my father had a little Christian store he ran for decades before the Communists shut it down. When war broke out with Japan, we ran into Gladys on more than one occasion. She was taking care of so many kids!"

Lost in thought, Grandma Lucy continued to speak of her time in Shanghai during the Sino-Japanese War. Stories of bombings, narrow escapes from death, heroic ventures her father undertook to help the injured, the selfless sacrifices her mother made to assist the war orphans.

"Of course, she never took in as many as Gladys," Grandma Lucy remarked with a smile that lit up her whole face and pushed her spectacles up on her cheeks. "But she did what God called her to, which is all he expects from each one of us, isn't it?"

Kennedy nodded, even though her mind was still back in war-torn Shanghai where Grandma Lucy had recounted stories of fires and destruction as readily as if she were talking about Sunday picnics in Central Park.

"And what about you?" she finally asked. "You say you're in medical school?"

"Pre-med," Kennedy corrected and spent the next few minutes answering questions about life as an undergrad student at Harvard.

"And are you part of a good church body over there?"

"Yeah." Kennedy didn't admit that she only made it to St. Margaret's once or twice a month, fearing it might make Grandma Lucy rethink Kennedy's previous claim of being a true *born-again* believer.

"That's good." Grandma Lucy nodded sagely. "I ask because that grandson of mine I just visited, he graduated from Harvard a few years ago, and it filled him with so many idolatrous, liberal views of God and religion and the world." She sighed. "He's a great boy, don't get me wrong. Has a heart bigger than most Christians who fill the churches across this country. Gets worked up over injustice and actually does something about it. Just to give you an example, before he left for work in Asia, he was in Detroit of all places, interviewing parents about this issue they're having in the education system there. The schools, they're falling apart. Not just the system, I mean the actual buildings are falling apart. One school's pipes were so bad, they were leaking lead into the drinking fountains. Had been going on for years before anyone fixed it. Just terrible. And then this whole big mess over the Brown Elementary School. You heard about that whole controversy, I'm sure."

"Actually, no." Kennedy tried not to sound embarrassed at the confession. She'd been so busy with her studies that if her dad didn't send her a link from one of his conservative news sites or Pastor Carl didn't say anything about it from the pulpit, she'd never hear about a particular current event. Especially not one from as far away as Detroit.

Grandma Lucy shook her head. "Terrible thing. I don't have all the facts. You'd have to talk to Ian about that. But it has something to do with them closing down one elementary school and merging it with another. Well, that was the plan. But the school they needed to shut down was mostly minorities, and the one they were going to merge with was more upper-class, and those parents got themselves all worked up. Made such a stink that the school district decided to build a new school for the poor kids instead, except the site they were planning to build on was in a bad part of town. I'm not talking crime. That's bad just about everywhere in Detroit from what I hear.

"But where they planned the new building, the land itself was no good. All kind of contaminants in the soil, toxic waste from chemical factories. Except the parents of these students, they weren't like the upper-class folks. They're working families, lots of single parents who are at their jobs during the day and can't attend meetings and forums. Even the ones who have time, a lot of them don't speak English well and they're too intimidated to stand up for themselves. So my grandson, he went and documented everything, got some statements from the families and a few other community members to show just how bad things had gotten.

"He sold it to one of the major networks, had it all lined up to air on national television, but then that night some big breaking story took its spot. Something about a murdered politician if I remember right, and that hogged the news for the next week or two until it was past back-to-school season and his network contact said nobody wanted to think about the education system anymore.

"He was pretty upset, obviously, not because of the money or anything, but because he believed in what these parents were going through. Really felt for them, I mean. He told me what he hated most was seeing how the school district gave in to intimidation when it came from the upper-class folks. The rich ones had the clout they needed to make the right kind of noise, but these minority families — the ones whose kids are going to suffer most in this new school they're building — they don't get a say at all. He thought he was giving them a voice with his camera, but it never even aired." She sighed. "He's got such a sensitive soul, I know God can use him for mighty things if he only gives his life to the Lord."

"It sounds like God's already using him," Kennedy suggested, but Grandma Lucy wasn't listening.

"I pray every day for that boy to come back to Christ. And now he's off travelling around Asia. Same thing. Human rights abuses, refugee crises. Always ready to speak up for the downtrodden and oppressed. So he's off to China with his camera but without the Holy Spirit to guide him. I gave him a Bible, and I told him I'd be praying for him. You know, that's all any of us can do in these situations, right? What about that roommate of yours? Is she born again?"

Kennedy kept her voice low, glad that Willow was sufficiently distracted. "I don't think so."

Grandma Lucy stared over her spectacles. "I take it you've witnessed to her by now?"

Kennedy glanced at Willow, who was snuggled up by Ray so they could share the same screen. "Well, I ..."

"You can't ever be ashamed of the gospel," Grandma Lucy interrupted. "Your roommate ... I can tell by the way she carries herself, that blue hair, those long earrings, that she's looking for something."

Kennedy wasn't sure you could discern that much about the state of a stranger's soul at first glance, but she didn't say anything. Something in Grandma Lucy's words had snuck past Kennedy's conversational barriers and found its mark in a conscience already ridden with guilt.

A year and a half sharing the same three-hundred square feet, and what had she done with that time? How many opportunities had she lost, opportunities to share the gospel with Willow, who was hurting, longing for more out of life whether or not her hair color had anything to do with her spiritual condition?

On the one hand, Kennedy was certain that if she were

to bring up God or salvation, Willow would go off on one of her tirades against religion. So what was the point? Willow said once that Kennedy was the only Christian she could stand to be around because she never tried to convert anyone. If Kennedy started preaching the gospel every minute of the day, telling Willow she was a sinner in danger of the fires of hell, that would only confirm her assumption that all Christians are judgmental jerks.

But even though her silence on the subject kept the peace between them, was that in Willow's best interest? Kennedy thought about the missionaries she'd been reading about in those biographies: Hudson Taylor, David Livingstone, Amy Carmichael. The Chinese called Gladys Aylward a foreign devil and threw mud at her the first day she stepped foot on foreign soil. But she had remained faithful to God's call and ended up leading hundreds to Christ.

Kennedy had never had mud thrown at her, had never been called horrid names, but maybe that was because she'd kept her faith so hidden. She thought about the refugees her parents trained to send back to North Korea as underground missionaries. How many of them would suffer imprisonment or death as a result of their witness? And here was Kennedy, scared of mentioning God because she didn't want to annoy her roommate.

Were her priorities that askew? Or was she just doing what God wanted her to do? What was it that Grandma Lucy had said earlier, something about nobody having to do more than God asked them to. Maybe Kennedy's job was to prove to Willow that not all Christians are out solely to win more converts or smugly judge sinful behavior. Maybe that's all God expected of her.

But how would Willow ever get saved if she never heard the gospel? Kennedy didn't like the guilt trip, Grandma Lucy's insinuation that if she really was a *born-again* believer she should have converted her roommate by now or else died trying like the martyrs of old.

Grandma Lucy laid her hand on Kennedy's forearm. "Now, you tell me your roommate's name, and I'm going to add her to my prayer list. Then I'll give you my phone number and you can let me know when she's been born again, all right?"

Kennedy sighed. "Her name's Willow."

Grandma Lucy pulled a tattered notebook out of her purse. "Willow," she repeated. "Oh, dear. She'll be one of the last ones, I'm afraid." She smiled and explained, "I keep my list alphabetized, so when I'm going to sleep I don't forget who's next on the list. I always start with my granddaughter Alayna and make my way down from there.

The good news is by the time I get to the Ws, I'll be nice and warmed up. If I haven't fallen asleep, that is."

Grandma Lucy's eyes twinkled, but Kennedy couldn't tell if she were making a joke or not. She didn't have time to wonder long before the bearded man in the turban jumped out of his chair with a startling shout.

"What's he think he's doing?" muttered the Seahawks fan with the BO. Several other passengers turned their heads as well.

The traveler pounded his fist into his seatback and yelled something frantic in Arabic.

The man in Carhartts stepped out of the bathroom and stood frozen in the aisle. BO Dude lowered his head onto his tray table and covered it with his hands as if he were a first-grader in an earthquake drill.

The man in the turban yelled aggressively, waving his hands in the air as if to emphasize a point.

"Get down," BO Dude hissed to Kennedy. "That maniac is about to take over the plane."

CHAPTER 5

Kennedy swallowed as the flight attendant behind her grabbed the phone from the wall. "Captain, this is Tracy," she whispered, and then her voice fell so Kennedy couldn't hear anymore. She glanced over at Willow, whose face had fallen ghastly white.

All sorts of horrific scenarios ran through Kennedy's mind. The man pulling a machine gun out from his billowing garments and raining lead on the entire cabin. Or revealing an armory of bombs and explosive taped across his chest and demanding entrance to the cockpit. That couldn't be it, though, could it? There were security measures. Metal detectors. TSA agents. He couldn't have boarded their plane if he was that dangerous, could he?

BO Dude turned in his seat, still covering his head and laying low. "We've got to take him down now," he hissed back to Willow's friend. "It's the only way. We take him down, or we don't get off this plane alive."

"Wait a minute," Ray protested.

The Seahawks fan had already unbuckled himself. "I'm telling you, it's either do something now, or we all end up blown to bits."

Kennedy thought back to the mother who had warned her family to get off the plane before takeoff. None of this could be happening, could it? Even her dad, as paranoid as he was, had never given her any hint of what to do in the event of a skyjacking.

"Stay in your seat, young man."

Kennedy was surprised at Grandma Lucy's authoritative voice.

"Turn up your hearing aid," BO Dude replied. "When a terrorist starts shouting in Arabic on a crowded plane, he's not asking for a bag of peanuts."

Grandma Lucy stood. She was short enough that she didn't have to stoop to keep from hitting her head on the fixture above. "No, he's not. And he's not speaking Arabic, either. It's Dari, which means he's from Afghanistan, and he's saying that there's something wrong with his father. It sounds like he might be having a heart attack."

She nodded at a male flight attendant who knelt down in front of the robed man and was checking his pulse with his fingers on the side of his throat. Kennedy let out her breath and felt sheepish for how quickly she had assumed the man must be a terrorist. So much for being against racial profiling.

Willow let out a forced laugh, and she and Ray went back to their movie.

The flight attendant Tracy who had been whispering on the phone now addressed the whole airplane over the PA system. "We have a medical situation on board and need everyone to remain seated. If you are a medical professional willing to offer assistance, please inform one of us on the flight crew."

Grandma Lucy reached out to stop the woman as she passed down the aisle. "I'm willing to help."

"Do you have medical training?" Tracy asked.

"No, but I speak a little Dari."

"Ok, come with me. We'll probably need to get him to the back of the cabin anyway. We have oxygen back here, and the AED if he needs it."

Grandma Lucy followed Tracy to the Afghani family in the front of the cabin. Kennedy wondered what it would be like in seven years when she had her medical degree and could offer assistance in an emergency like this. She still wasn't sure what field of medicine she wanted to go into. Pediatrics was out. She'd never felt comfortable around kids, and the thought of dealing with children with any disease more severe than the common cold was downright depressing. She figured surgery would be interesting, but she didn't love the idea of bending over cut-open bodies ten hours a stretch. She'd probably start off in internal medicine and decide to specialize from there once something caught her attention. She'd had her eye on immunology for some time now, but expecting her to choose a specialty now was like asking a seventh-grader to pick their college major. It just didn't work that way. How would she know what she enjoyed or what she was good at without a few more years of experience? Thankfully, nobody was in a rush except for Kennedy herself, who would be happy to have a more definitive ten-year plan than *graduate from medical school.*

At some point, of course, she wanted to marry. But when? If she was too busy to date anyone seriously as an undergrad, there was no way she'd find the time for a relationship in med school. Her residency would be even worse. Once she was ready to settle down with anyone, would there be any decent men still single?

Dominic was a good guy. She wished he enjoyed reading fiction so they had more to talk about. But even though she enjoyed her time with him and experienced a little girlish excitement when she'd get ready for one of their quasi-dates, she always felt like she had to prove something to him. Prove that she was spiritually fit enough to be in a relationship with a police chaplain. Prove that she was mature enough to go out with someone who had already been married and widowed before his thirtieth birthday. Prove to herself that she wasn't at least a tiny bit uncomfortable when they were together, struggling to find things to talk about that weren't God, the Bible, and Kennedy's life as a missionary kid.

She couldn't remember why she was thinking about Dominic by the time the Afghani son helped his ashen-faced father stumble to the snack station in the back of the cabin. Two flight attendants, Grandma Lucy, and a middle-aged man in a fancy suit hovered over him.

His son repeated the same word over and over.

"He says he can't breathe," Grandma Lucy translated.

"Sit him down here."

The well-dressed passenger knelt, checking the patient's pulse while Tracy strapped an oxygen mask across his face. Kennedy had a hard time focusing on their words as Grandma Lucy was standing over them holding a conversation of her own. With one hand lifted to the heavens and one aimed down toward the patient's head, Grandma Lucy raised her voice.

"God, you know this man's needs. You know his history. You know his body. You know exactly what's wrong and exactly how to fix it. And I believe in Jesus' name that you want to heal him. And so we pray for your healing. We pray for your …"

"Here's the medical kit, doctor." A male flight attendant passed the case to the man in the suit, who flung it open and rummaged around. The patient's son gripped the doctor's hand and repeated the same phrase with an urgency in his voice that made Kennedy's lungs seize up in anxiety.

"No pulse-ox?" the doctor asked, pressing against the patient's fingertips and frowning at the results.

The patient signaled to his throat wildly.

"I know." The doctor spoke softly but couldn't keep a certain edge of tension out of his voice.

"This is all we have," Tracy explained apologetically, while Grandma Lucy lifted her head once more and continued her prayer.

"Lord, this doctor needs equipment. And you've promised that when we ask for anything in your name, you'll give it to us, and so we ask in the name of Jesus for whatever he needs to help his patient be healed. And we claim that healing, Lord. We claim it in the name of Jesus. We claim his …"

"Ok, ma'am." Tracy set aside the phone she'd been talking into and gently pushed on Grandma Lucy's shoulder. "I think the professionals can take it from here."

"Actually," the doctor frowned, "I might need some kind of health history. Maybe she should stick around, only more quietly."

If Grandma Lucy was upset by his request, she didn't show it. She kept the same position but this time only moved her lips instead of giving free reign to her words. To judge by her facial expressions, however, the enforced silence only increased the fervency of her prayers.

The adult son continued to shoot rapid-fire questions at the doctor who tried assuring him in English that he was doing the best he could.

Tracy hung up the phone. "We're only twenty minutes from an airport with a hospital nearby."

"I don't know if he'll make it that long." The doctor yanked a stethoscope out of the medical kit.

"We do have an AED on board," Tracy told him.

Grandma Lucy opened her eyes and declared definitively, "He's not having a heart attack."

Tracy sighed. "Ma'am, I think maybe if you have a seat, we can ask for your help if we need it."

"It's not a heart attack," she repeated.

The doctor lowered the stethoscope. "No, it's not his heart. She's right. Sounds like pneumonia. Can you ask the son if his father has a history of lung disease?"

"I don't know the word." Grandma Lucy frowned. "But I'll try to come up with something." She asked a question in Dari and listened to the son's quick reply.

"I can't understand all of it," she admitted, "but he said something about medicine for a cough he's had."

"Medicine?" the doctor repeated. "Ask him if he has the medicine with him. Ask him if it's a new prescription."

Grandma Lucy nodded. It took a round or two of charades before the son understood what the doctor wanted. He hurried back toward his seat to find his father's carry-on.

"Should I tell the captain to land?" Tracy asked.

"Let's plan on it," the doctor answered. "But if we're dealing with an allergic reaction of some kind, we might be able to handle it here." He pulled a syringe out of the medical kit and checked the label.

The son hurried back up the aisle and thrust a pill bottle into the doctor's empty hand.

"This is what he's been taking?" he asked. Grandma Lucy didn't have to translate. The son pointed to the pills, then to his father and pantomimed dumping out a tablet and swallowing.

The doctor squinted at the label. "Penicillin. Probably for the pneumonia. Can you ask him if his father's ever had this drug before?"

Grandma Lucy didn't have time to ask before the patient shot out his hand and grabbed the doctor by the wrist. He motioned to his throat.

"His trachea's swollen shut." The doctor swept his arms to the sides to make more room. He uncapped the syringe. "Let's roll." He plunged the needle into the man's leg before anyone had time to look away.

Kennedy grimaced but still leaned toward them. Waiting. Would the medicine work? How did the doctor know he'd given him the right amount?

The patient's eyes were wide with fear. His son knelt beside him, muttering what sounded like a prayer under his breath.

The doctor pulled the syringe away. More waiting.

"Shouldn't it be working by now?" Tracy asked.

The doctor frowned but didn't reply.

"Help him, Jesus," Grandma Lucy whispered.

The doctor listened to his heart once more. "Better get that AED ready."

Kennedy wanted to pry her eyes away but couldn't. She added a silent prayer on top of Grandma Lucy's. *Please, Jesus ...*

The man gasped in a wheezy breath. His son grasped his hand and let out an exultant proclamation.

"You're going to be ok," the doctor told him, and Grandma Lucy began loudly declaring her thanks to God.

The doctor listened to the man's lungs for a full minute before he put the stethoscope down again. "I think it's safe to say the worst is over. An allergic reaction." He looked at Grandma Lucy. "Tell the son his dad can't have these pills anymore. He'll have to take something else for his cough."

"So he's ok?" Tracy asked, reaching for the phone again.

"Let's keep him on oxygen for a little while longer, just to be safe. Make sure someone stays back here with him. When his shot wears off, he might go through the same set of symptoms again. I imagine if he feels better in half an hour or so, he can go back to his seat as long as his son keeps watch over him the whole time."

"So you don't think we need to divert the flight?" Tracy asked.

"As long as there's another EpiPen ready in that kit, we should be golden."

Tracy relayed the news to the captain on the phone, and the doctor returned to first class without another word. Grandma Lucy sat down next to the patient and struck up a conversation with his son. They had to repeat themselves several times, but they must have been communicating somewhat effectively because at one point they both laughed. A few minutes later, Grandma Lucy pulled a travel-size Bible from the pocket of her sweater and handed it to him. After a few more exchanges, she stood up with much more agility than Kennedy expected from someone her age.

"So he's all right?" Kennedy asked.

"Just fine," Grandma Lucy answered as she sat down by her with a subdued groan. "Hallelujah, praise the Lord. He's going to be just fine."

BO Dude leaned across the aisle and asked, "What's that mask they got on his face?"

"Some extra oxygen," Grandma Lucy explained, her eyes still lifted heavenward in rapture.

"Fabulous," he grumbled. "Who's great idea was it to put them both by a tank of explosive gas?" He turned around to shoot Ray an angry glare and muttered, "Told you we should have taken him down when we had the chance."

"You have nothing to fear from a nice gentleman like Mr. Wahidi." Grandma Lucy was probably two-hundred pounds lighter than the Seahawks fan, but she looked down at him as if he'd been half her size. "He's very polite and has just emigrated to the US."

"Stinking refugees," BO Dude hissed, tossing a few more colorful epithets into his salad mix of insults.

"Not a refugee," Grandma Lucy corrected, "an emigre, invited here by the United States government. I believe his son said he's a scientist."

The Seahawks fan let out a disgusted scoff but thankfully didn't say any more.

A few minutes later, Tracy walked back carrying a plate of cheesecake bites. "These are from first class, but the crew and I wanted to offer them to you to thank you for your help."

Grandma Lucy didn't take the pastries. "You better save these for that doctor. He's the one who did the real assisting, not me."

The flight attendant lowered her voice. "He's already in first class." She smiled and set the snacks on Grandma Lucy's tray table.

"Well, there's more than enough." Grandma Lucy handed out the desserts, one for Kennedy, two for Willow and Ray, and the last for BO Dude.

"Don't you want some?" Kennedy asked.

Grandma Lucy dipped her finger into Kennedy's strawberry swirl topping. "You don't mind if I share a little with you, right?"

Kennedy stared as Grandma Lucy licked her finger with a delighted smile. No longer hungry, she insisted Grandma Lucy finish the whole thing.

"How do you know that language they were speaking?" Kennedy asked when the desserts were gone.

Grandma Lucy reclined her chair and stretched her legs out beneath the empty seat in front of her.

"I did some mission work in Afghanistan in the seventies. I went over there to teach English, but God opened so many doors for me to share the gospel, too. All in all, I spent two years there, and I knew the language pretty well by the time I came back. I got more practice in Washington once Russia invaded Afghanistan, and I started a ministry assisting refugees, helping them get housing in the States, fill out job applications, learn English. It was a full-time job even though it was just volunteer work. And God kept opening doors to lead people to Christ. I had to quit after my daughter died. I moved in with my son-in-law to help raise the children."

"That's terrible. What happened?"

Grandma Lucy lowered her head into her oversized purse and dug around. "Killed by a drunk driver. Left behind two kids, a boy and a girl. Ian's the one I told you about, the one I just visited. Poor guy. Broke his little heart."

Kennedy tried to fathom the horror of losing a parent in such a terrible tragedy. "How old was he?"

"Just five. You know, I think that's part of the reason why he turned his back on God. It was a horrible thing to happen, and him being so young." She shook her head and started digging through her carry-on bag. "Oh. Here it is." She pulled out a handkerchief with cowboys printed on it in bright reds and blues. "Don't mind me," she said as she draped the cloth over her entire face. "It's time for my nap, and if I do say so myself, I think I deserve a good long one."

Kennedy didn't answer. She was tired as well. Grandma Lucy adjusted once or twice in her seat and then grew perfectly still. Kennedy glanced over at Willow and Ray, who were still absorbed in their movie. Oh, well. Kennedy would have plenty of time to spend with her roommate in Alaska. It wasn't as if she'd miss out on an hour of talk time on the plane.

She picked up her Gladys Aylward biography and by the time Grandma Lucy's slow, rhythmic snoring reached her ears, she had finished the book.

CHAPTER 6

T minus 36 minutes

Kennedy didn't know what to do to pass the time. Grandma Lucy was asleep. Willow and Ray were in the middle of their movie. She would have never guessed it, but traveling to Willow's home in Alaska was just as exhausting of an ordeal as getting to her parents' home in Yanji, China. After they reached Anchorage, they'd book a hotel for the night before Willow's dad picked them up for the four-hour drive to Glennallen. All in all, it would be more than twenty-four hours from the time they left campus until they arrived at Willow's home. She hoped she wouldn't be too tired.

Something Grandma Lucy said now sat like curdled milk in Kennedy's gut. Why hadn't she witnessed to Willow? Was she just waiting for the perfect time? Knowing her roommate, she doubted that would ever come. So what was she supposed to do — risk alienating her only real friend on campus to share a message she was certain Willow didn't want to hear, or stay quiet and do her best to ignore the fact that her roommate might die without ever learning the good news of salvation?

It was supposed to be easy. From the time she was seven or eight, Kennedy's dad taught her the four spiritual laws, the ABCs of salvation, the Romans Road of witnessing. And what good had it ever done her? She just wasn't the type to butt her way into random conversations and ask, "Do you know what it means to be saved?" She'd had the sinner's prayer memorized for a decade, but for what purpose? She'd never shared it with anyone, certainly never prayed it with anyone since that night when she was five and climbed up on her dad's lap and told him she wanted to become a Christian. She'd already said the prayer a dozen times or more in Sunday school by then, but she knew it was a way to get her dad to let her stay up late. He'd made such a big deal of her so-called conversion, giving her a brand new Bible with her spiritual birthday imprinted inside, taking her out for donuts to celebrate before church the next day, beaming proudly when he told Mrs. Lindgren about the choice she'd just made. Kennedy remembered wearing an itchy dress and squirming uncomfortably because she'd raised her hand to pray the prayer in Sunday school so many different times by then and didn't want her teacher to ruin her dad's enthusiasm by letting out their little secret.

And so Kennedy had been "converted," even though she couldn't remember a single moment in her childhood when she hadn't understood that Jesus died in order to forgive her sins. If she hadn't wanted to get out of an early bedtime that night fourteen years ago, she'd be just the same Christian she was today, right? So what was the big deal?

Well, maybe God was speaking to her heart about Willow. Isn't that how Hudson Taylor knew he was supposed to go to China, how David Livingstone knew he was called to Africa? When she read about the experiences of these missionaries, she always expected *The Call* to feel exciting. Invigorating. The conviction that God was right beside her, that he had a fabulous plan for her life, that he was going to do incredible things through her. She didn't think her mission assignment from the Lord would come in the form of nagging self-doubt and guilt.

She sighed. Well, if God wanted her to tell Willow about him, she'd do it, right? Isn't that what it meant to be obedient to Christ no matter what the cost? And if Willow threw a fit, well, God would just have to take care of the details, wouldn't he? What was the worst that could happen? It's not like Willow would uninvite her to her home and leave her stranded in Anchorage over Christmas.

Kennedy stared at the picture of Gladys Aylward on the back of her book. Such a quiet-looking, unassuming woman. Kind of like Grandma Lucy, who still snored comfortably next to her. Grandma Lucy certainly wouldn't be afraid of sharing the gospel with someone like Willow. But she also had less to lose. Grandma Lucy wouldn't have to see Willow every day for the rest of the semester, wouldn't have to live in the same dorm until summer break.

Maybe it was easier to share the gospel with people you didn't know. Maybe that's why those pamphlet pushers did what they did, why certain sects sent their congregants out ringing doorbells. If you get laughed at and have the door slammed in your face, are you that much worse off for it other than a little bit of a bruised ego?

Maybe Kennedy could bargain with God. If not Willow, what about the dozen students she knew by name or sight but didn't have to live with for the rest of her sophomore year? What about the girl in organic chem lab who was always burning herself on the Bunsen burner, or the leader of that campus singing group Willow auditioned for? The upperclassman had been ruder than Ebenezer Scrooge himself when he said her roommate didn't have the kind of stage presence they were looking for. If anyone at Harvard needed the gospel, it was him.

Yeah, God. Send me there instead.

She hoped the guilt would let up, but of course it didn't. She searched her memory for a Bible verse that would let her off the hook. *God loves a cheerful giver*? If Kennedy wasn't feeling very cheerful about giving herself a mouthful of humble pie, she shouldn't bother until her heart was in a better place, right? Or what about that verse where Jesus said he knew his sheep and his sheep knew him. If Willow was destined to be part of God's family, wouldn't God find a way to save her without any help?

Then again, isn't that exactly what the veteran pastor said to Hudson Taylor about his passion to carry the gospel to the Chinese interior? "When God pleases to convert the heathen, he'll do it without the help of people like you and me." Kennedy had been incensed when she read the minister's cavalier response, appalled that Christians in the 1800s could have resorted to such ugly, calloused excuses. But was Kennedy doing anything better? If God wanted Willow saved, he'd do it with or without Kennedy's help. Isn't that what she'd just told herself? Well, what if she was wrong?

She didn't know how it all worked out, didn't know what the Bible meant when it said that God *chose* some for salvation in some passages but in other passages talked about him *willing that none should perish*. Those were theological matters people like her dad or Dominic could discuss until they were hoarse with laryngitis, and it probably wouldn't make a hair's width of difference in Kennedy's day-to-day life.

But what if there weren't just people destined to salvation and people doomed to perish? What if there were regular, average individuals who would ask Jesus to forgive their sins if they had the right information, except nobody told them the actual path to heaven? She thought about a verse they read at a home-based Bible study Dominic invited her to a few weeks ago. After announcing woe on certain cities, Jesus declared if the miracles that had been performed there had been performed in Sodom and Gomorrah, they would have repented. It came from somewhere in Matthew, although Kennedy could only guess what chapter. But it was clear that there were some cities that would have repented if they'd been given a decent enough chance. And if that could be said of cities, couldn't that be said of individuals as well?

Something was changing in Kennedy as she read so many missionary stories. Apart from the inevitable guilt she experienced every time she thought about how many people she wasn't sharing the gospel with, she found a deeper conviction to try to pray better. She didn't quite know what that meant, and she was sure she was floundering just as poorly as she ever had, but at least she was more aware now of her own shortcomings and need for growth. She certainly wouldn't measure up to people like George Mueller, the orphanage director whose entire life was a story of God's inexhaustible providence coupled with man's boundless faith. She recalled how he kept a list of unsaved friends. He persevered for decades interceding for dozens, maybe hundreds of different people until they finally came to Christ. A few months after he died, the last person on George Mueller's prayer list became a Christian.

That's what Kennedy needed. To pray for Willow. Forget about alienating her roommate by forcing her into spiritual conversations. Pray for Willow and see what God did.

It sounded like a solid plan.

It also sounded like a pathetic cop-out.

Well, she was trying. God must be able to test her heart and see that much, at least.

She looked at her roommate. Willow was gorgeous, with a certain flamboyant style that attracted attention wherever she went. No wonder Ray had sought her out instead of someone like Kennedy, who felt herself about as dumpy as Bob Cratchit's wife in *A Christmas Carol*.

In general, Kennedy wasn't a fan of unnatural hair colors, but there was something so stunning about Willow's multilayered dye job. The highlights rippled in and out until her whole head was like a box of crayons in all shades of blue. There was an iridescent shine that made her hair glow with radiance.

Yes, Kennedy was definitely Emily Cratchit in comparison. Of course Willow would be the one getting the attention. Kennedy shouldn't be jealous. It was miraculous that Dominic took enough of an interest in her to invite her out a few times over the past semester. Even so, their few trips together hardly constituted a dating relationship, which she wouldn't have time for anyway, not with her studies and dual lab classes. Besides, there was something distant about Dominic. Maybe it was just a personality trait, but after a whole semester, she still didn't feel like she knew him more than she did the first night they met. She'd never seen him angry. Never seen him sad except for one weekend after he had to tell two frantic parents that the investigators had recovered their little girl's drowned body. Even then, he was mostly stoic as he related the horrible events.

Kennedy's mom was glad to hear that Kennedy had found someone, even though at first she'd been a little concerned about the age difference. More than anything, Kennedy got the sense her mom was just glad that Dominic didn't have HIV like other people who'd come into her life in the past.

Sometimes Kennedy wondered why she spent time with Dominic at all. It's not like she'd be ready to settle down and marry in another year or two. He'd be nearly forty by the time she graduated med school. There was no way she expected him to wait that long, even if he was the kind of guy she could picture one day settling down with.

She caught herself staring at Willow's new friend Ray, wondering how old he was, wondering what kind of women caught his eye, if he was the kind of teacher all the girls at his school giggled about at their lunch tables.

While she was lost in thought, he stood up and stretched his legs in the aisle. "It's been great visiting. I wish I could stay longer. I don't think I've seen a Freddie flick since I was a teenager."

Willow's smile was as dazzling as always. "Well then, you were long overdue. Come back in a little bit and we can watch the rest."

"Yeah, sure. If I finish grading these geometry tests before we land, I'd like that a lot." He turned to look at Kennedy, who hoped he hadn't noticed her staring. "You can have your seat back now. Sorry I stole your friend for so long."

Kennedy made some sort of awkward reply and just barely got out of her seat without tripping into him in the process.

"That was smooth," Willow teased when Kennedy sat down next to her.

Kennedy rolled her eyes. After a year and a half sharing the same tiny dorm, she was used to Willow's sarcastic sense of humor, but she didn't have the patience for it. Not right now.

"So what'd you and Granny yak about over there?" Willow asked. "For a while there, it looked like you'd found yourself a new best buddy."

Kennedy didn't know why she felt defensive of Grandma Lucy all of a sudden. She did what she could to change the subject. "Ray seems real nice."

Willow lifted one shoulder in a shrug. "He is." She brushed her blue bangs out of her eyes. "A little bit too nice for my taste, but it was fine."

Kennedy didn't know what to say next. She hoped Christmas vacation with Willow's family wouldn't be this awkward. On campus, they never had a hard time coming up with topics to talk about. That was because something was always going on. Willow had new plays to rehearse, new theater friends to gossip about. Kennedy was always reading a different classic, and since Willow wanted to be as cultured and literate as she could without actually having to sit down and read anything, she often asked Kennedy for the abridged versions. But now, with half the day left just to get to Seattle, Kennedy was afraid they'd already run out of conversation topics. It wasn't as if she could talk about people like Gladys Aylward and Hudson Taylor, missionaries who Willow would insist destroyed indigenous cultures with their colonialist zeal and ethnocentrism.

She sighed. How was she supposed to witness when she could barely hold a simple conversation? God must have other plans for Willow. If she was going to hear the gospel message, it would have to come from somebody else. Wasn't it Jesus himself who lamented that a prophet is never accepted in his hometown? That's what was going on here. The two girls were just too close. Willow had seen Kennedy at her worst, had walked with her through the most painful moments of her post-traumatic stress flare-ups, through losing her best friend and lab partner last year after making a complete idiot of herself on a live news segment ...

"What's going on in that brain of yours, genius?" Willow asked.

Kennedy was glad she didn't have to answer truthfully. "Nothing really. I guess I'm just tired." She looked over at Willow, who didn't respond. Kennedy tried to figure out who she was staring at. "What are you ..."

"Shhh." Willow grabbed her arm and didn't let go. "Quiet," she hissed.

"What is it?" Kennedy whispered.

Willow leaned in until their heads touched. "That guy there. The one with that gaudy Hawaiian shirt."

Kennedy stared. "What about him?"

"Lean over this way."

Kennedy didn't see anything out of the ordinary besides the fact that he was so overweight. That and the way his teenage daughter sat so close to him. Still, Kennedy had flown internationally at that age and probably fell asleep on her dad's shoulder half a dozen times or more.

"That is so wrong." Willow reached up and turned on her alert light.

Tracy was stocking a snack tray behind them. "I'll be right there."

"What is it?" Kennedy asked as unease crept up her spine like a hairy tarantula.

The flight attendant bent over toward Willow and turned off the light. "What can I do for you?"

"That man in the Hawaiian shirt." Willow nodded with her head.

The woman frowned. "What about him?"

Willow's penciled eyebrows narrowed dramatically. "He was pulling her hair back. Like this." She snatched Kennedy's ponytail and gave it a half-hearted tug. "Like he was threatening her."

The woman paused and glanced at Kennedy. "You saw it, too?"

"No, but I ... Well, the angle's different here, and it ..."

Tracy let out her breath and donned a plastered smile that only slightly concealed her annoyance. Or maybe she was just tired. "Well, if you see anything else suspicious ..."

"Something's not right." Willow shook her head. "Something's definitely wrong over there."

Tracy gently touched Willow's shoulder. "I'll tell the other attendants to keep their eyes open, ok?"

Willow ran her fingers through her glossy hair. "There's got to be something ..."

The woman leaned a little closer. "Thanks for bringing it to our attention. You did the right thing."

Kennedy couldn't tell if she was saying what she needed to say to end the conversation or if there was genuine concern behind her voice. How many people did these flight attendants come across each day? She'd never thought about it before, but it seemed like it must be one of the grossest, most thankless jobs imaginable. Cleaning up used barf bags, listening to squealing babies, reacting during any number of medical emergencies …

"Oh, before you go," Kennedy piped up.

"Yes?" Now the exhaustion in Tracy's voice was unmistakable even though she still tried a winning attempt at a smile.

"How's the patient doing? The one who needed the extra oxygen earlier? Is he ok?"

The smiled warmed for a brief moment. "I can't discuss that, but I can tell you that if we thought he was in any danger, the pilot would have diverted the flight a long time ago to get him to a hospital." She straightened her crisp uniform. "I'll be around in just a few minutes with drinks."

Neither girl answered. Willow continued to stare at the fat man and his teenage daughter. Kennedy tried but couldn't pinpoint anything abnormal or suspicious about either of them.

After a few more minutes, Willow pulled out her phone. "How about a game of Scrabble?" she asked.

Kennedy felt like she must be letting God down every minute of the day. She couldn't talk to her roommate about Jesus. She couldn't tell her about the way to salvation or the price he paid so her sins could be forgiven. But she could play a Scrabble knockoff on her roommate's smartphone and wrack up three or four hundred points by the time the score was settled.

Kennedy smiled even though she knew her expression would be even less convincing than the flight attendant's.

"Sure. You go first."

CHAPTER 7

T minus 11 minutes

"I don't even know why I bother to play you." Willow sulked dramatically.

Less than half an hour after they started their game, Kennedy was declared the winner by fifty-seven points. Her highest word, *quench*, had surged her score ahead. Willow never had the chance to recover.

Kennedy wadded up her pretzel bag and shoved it into her empty cup. Why hadn't she thought to pack a few snacks to take with her on the plane? They would touch down in Detroit soon, but they wouldn't get off until Seattle, where she hoped they'd have time to grab some real food.

"I'm going to use the bathroom." Kennedy unbuckled.

"You'll have to go up front," Willow told her. "That guy in the Carhartts locked himself in a few minutes ago."

"Again?" Kennedy asked, remembering how backed up the bathroom line had grown earlier in the flight. Oh, well. It would be a good idea to stretch her legs anyway. What was that her dad was always worried about? Embolisms midflight or something like that. Kennedy seriously doubted she was in any danger of developing blood clots at her age, but she'd end up with a whole body full of sore and achy muscles if she didn't move around a little bit.

She glanced across the aisle where Grandma Lucy still slept with the cowboy handkerchief covering her face. She hadn't joked when she said she'd earned herself a nap. In front of Willow, BO Dude was busy chewing his pencil and working on a crossword puzzle that only had four answers filled, with a glaring spelling mistake in the top row. Several seats ahead, Ray leaned over a stack of papers and was so busy with his quintessential red pen he didn't even notice her pass, or if he did, he didn't acknowledge her. The girl in the Bon Jovi shirt sat in front of him, and Kennedy slowed her pace so she could observe her longer without getting caught staring. Her father in his Hawaiian shirt had an arm around her, and the girl seemed a little squeamish, but that didn't mean a whole lot. How many teen girls did Kennedy know who wanted to be affectionate with their dads in public?

The girl twisted in her seat and looked back until her eyes locked with Kennedy's. There was something piercing in her expression that made Kennedy's breath catch in her trachea. Had Willow just made her paranoid, or was there something more to it? Something more sinister? There wasn't time to gawk in the aisle until she figured it out. She had to keep moving, but right as she was about to pass, the girl shot out her leg like a mischievous third grader trying to pull a prank on a friend.

Kennedy stumbled and grabbed the back of a seat for balance.

"Oh, I'm sorry." The girl leaned forward, grabbing Kennedy's hand. The haunting eyes never left hers. A flicker of resolve was replaced by fear as her father coughed up a loogie, which he noisily spat into his empty soda can.

"Are you ok?" the girl asked. Her eyes were wide.

Kennedy felt a sympathetic quivering in her core and shoved her fist into her pocket. She tried to sound confident and nodded. "I'm fine." She didn't dare dart her eyes to the father but added quickly for his benefit, "It was just an accident. I should have been paying better attention."

With that, she rushed past the last few rows, threw herself into the lavatory, and flung the lock down. Her hand was burning. The same hand the girl had grabbed after intentionally tripping Kennedy. The same hand the girl had thrust a crumpled napkin into. The same hand that trembled as Kennedy pulled it out of her pocket, unfolded the note, and read, *My name is Selena Weston. I'm being kidnapped.*

CHAPTER 8

T minus 7 minutes

Think. She had to think. Kennedy hadn't gotten into Harvard for her social graces or athletic skills. She had a brain somewhere beneath that skull and head of thick hair. She could figure this out. Come up with a plan.

The last thing she wanted to do was alert the fat man to anything suspicious. If he found out the girl had signaled for help, who knew what sort of trouble she'd be in? But how did the authorities handle situations like this in the middle of a flight? It wasn't as if Kennedy could simply call 911 and ask the dispatcher to send a few squad cars down to rescue an abducted teen. How had he gotten her on the plane in the first place? Weren't the TSA agents supposed to have an eye out for that sort of thing?

She had to let one of the flight attendants know, but she had to do it so the father — no, the abductor — wouldn't notice. Which meant that as soon as she was done in the bathroom, she'd have to walk down the aisle, right past Selena. She'd have to act so natural it would make Willow and all her theater friends applaud her performance if they knew what was going on. Then she'd give the note to Tracy in the back of the plane.

The plan would work. It would have to work.

Finding she no longer needed to pee, she exited the bathroom on unsteady legs. She'd already resolved not to look at Selena. Not to draw any further attention. She'd walk right by as if she didn't notice her there. If only her body would stop trembling.

She held onto the back of a seat for support and fixed her eyes on Ray, still bent fastidiously over his pile of math tests. Willow was most likely right. He was probably too much of a nice guy for her, if *nice guy* meant a respectable working man who had responsibilities that prevented him from partying hard seven nights a week.

He glanced up from his papers. "Hey there." He knitted his brows together. "Are you all right?"

Kennedy tilted her head up. "Just a little motion sick." It wasn't necessarily a lie.

He gave her a sympathetic frown. "Try some Ginger Ale."

She tried to keep focused on him, but her legs grew even more unsteady when she saw the man in the Hawaiian shirt leering at her.

"Is she the one?" he snarled at the teen.

Selena's eyes were wide with fear. Kennedy bit her lip. She tried to ignore his angry glare and focused on Selena, who winced as Hawaiian Shirt dug his fingers into the flesh of her arm. "That the one?" he demanded again.

Selena's eyes were sorrowful. Pleading. She gave a slight nod.

Kennedy's body sensed the danger before her gray matter could create a single coherent thought. The result was nearly complete paralysis. A surge of epinephrine raged throughout her system, begging Kennedy to flee, but there was nowhere to go. The aisle was too narrow. A step closer and she'd be within the abductor's reach.

She froze, while Ray the nice-guy math teacher cocked his head to the side like a curious puppy.

It was all the time Hawaiian Shirt needed to lunge out of his seat and grab Kennedy's arm. "Give me that paper, you piece of trash."

Tiny snippets of her self-defense lessons sped through her mind, reflexes that came about three seconds too late. She yanked her arm back. He only tightened his grip. She wrenched her hand down, trying to twist his forearm. He threw his body weight into her but didn't let go.

Kennedy knew she should call for help, but her breath had been startled out of her.

"Hey! Let go of her!" Ray bolted out of his seat and flung himself against Hawaiian Shirt, trying to grab his arms from behind.

A shrill screaming pierced Kennedy's ears. "Help!" Selena covered her head with her arms to shield herself from the scuffle. "Somebody, help."

Ray let out a loud *oof* as Hawaiian Shirt punched him in the gut. Kennedy realized she was free and tried to distance herself but ended up tripping on Selena's arm rest. She fell, clawing at the man who yanked her to her feet.

"Hold it!" An authoritative voice cracked through the cacophony.

More noise. More punches. She was so startled she couldn't even tell if she was hurt or not.

"Freeze."

Kennedy couldn't see who was talking. She could hardly even focus on who she was supposed to be fighting off. She found herself pounding her fists against someone significantly smaller than the fat man in the Hawaiian shirt. When her eyes finally focused, she saw she was beating Ray, who held her by both shoulders and was telling her she was safe.

Kennedy's whole body quivered uncontrollably. The

stress, the trauma, the anxiety she'd ignored during the fight raged through her system with the energy of a nuclear explosion.

"It's ok," Ray repeated as humiliating tears slipped down Kennedy's cheeks.

He held her a little closer, as if trying to offer reassurance without making it an official hug. "You're safe," he whispered and nodded toward a mustached man in a dark business suit who was about to cuff Hawaiian Shirt's hands behind his back.

"I don't even know that man," Selena was sobbing. "He told me he'd kill me if I didn't go with him."

Tracy wrapped her arm around the crying girl and ushered her to the front of the plane.

Kennedy reached out her arm for something to steady herself on.

"Easy," Ray said. "Here, let me walk you back to your seat."

"She was being kidnapped." Kennedy's brain refused to focus on more than one face at a time. She fought her way past the nauseating dizziness looking for Selena.

"It's ok," Ray assured her. "She's going to be fine. Everything's going to be just fine."

Kennedy sucked in a choppy breath and thought that

maybe in a few minutes she could believe Ray's assessment of their situation.

Something buzzed, and the captain addressed the cabin. "Well, folks, it looks like we had a little excitement back there. The good news is we'll be landing in Detroit in about twenty minutes. Let's show the flight attendants and air marshal on board our appreciation for working well under pressure to keep everybody safe."

Subdued applause sounded throughout the cabin until Hawaiian Shirt guffawed. "Safe?" He let out a soul-haunting chuckle. "That's what you think, chump."

He swung his head back until his skull smacked into the air marshal's face. Kennedy instinctively clutched Ray's arm as the man in the SVSU sweatshirt jumped into the aisle. In one swift motion, he grabbed the pistol from the marshal's holster, raised it above his head, and brought it down on his skull. A grotesque thud sounded above the hum of muffled cries.

The man in the sweatshirt kept the gun held high in the air. "This is your captain speaking. I suggest you buckle up."

CHAPTER 9

Kennedy glanced back at Willow, but she couldn't focus on her roommate before Ray pulled her into an empty seat. "Get down," he hissed in her ear.

"He's got a gun," shrieked a woman from the front of the plane. "Everyone watch out. He's got a gun."

Kennedy stared at the marshal's crumpled form, as if she could wake him up by sheer will power.

"Here's how it's gonna go." The SVSU man had his back to the emergency exit. His voice carried throughout the whole cabin. "You will all address me as General. This here is my lieutenant." He nodded at the fat man in the Hawaiian shirt. "You are now under our care and protection, got that?"

"What do you want?" squeaked the hysterical woman.

Kennedy's breath wheezed into her lungs when General leveled the gun in the direction of the speaker.

"What I want is silence," he boomed and then let his volume drop. "Silence and a little cooperation. You give me my space, you give me some respect, and we're all gonna get through this just fine. Got that?"

Kennedy didn't realize at first how badly she was trembling. She curled her legs up against her chest and leaned a little closer toward Ray.

"Who here's got a cell phone?" General asked as Lieutenant Hawaiian Shirt busied himself binding the unconscious air marshal's ankles and wrists with a roll of thick metal wire. "I said who's got a cell phone?" General repeated in a roar.

A few passengers tentatively raised their hands, but most like Kennedy held perfectly still. She heard BO Dude's voice in her mind. *We take him down, or we don't get off this plane alive.* She knew logically a whole cabin full of travelers could subdue two men. But the gun …

She looked to the back of the plane but all she could see of Willow was the top of her blue hair. Was she ok? Was she as terrified as Kennedy? What about Grandma Lucy? Was she asleep with the cowboy handkerchief draped over her eyes? Did she have any idea what was happening?

BO Dude sat with his arms crossed. "What're you gonna do? Pass around a pillowcase for us to dump our cells in like we're in some sort of action flick?"

Kennedy watched him, wished he'd get up and act. Take down the crazy man from SVSU, wherever that was.

A smile softened General's features momentarily. "I'm not gonna take your phones. In fact, I want you to pull them out. I've got something to say that some of you may want to record."

The PA system sounded. "This is the captain speaking. Yup, me again. And if you're a passenger who doesn't have a death wish, I suggest you buckle up."

High-pitched screams, including her own, drowned out Kennedy's other senses as the airplane tipped onto its side. Beside her, Ray fumbled with the safety belt to strap her in.

The plane dived forward. Kennedy squeezed her eyes shut, trying to calculate how long it would take a plane to freefall forty-thousand feet given a constant acceleration due to gravity. She couldn't keep any figures straight in her head.

The plane straightened again, and Kennedy opened her eyes. Apparently BO Dude had been the only passenger brave or senseless enough to get out of his seat and take advantage of the confusion to confront General. He landed one misplaced punch by General's ear before the plane lurched again and both men stumbled off balance. By then, General's fat lieutenant had joined the skirmish. He punched BO Dude in the jaw before the captain rolled the plane to the left.

Kennedy's shoulder was thrown against the window a moment before her head. She couldn't see anything, couldn't focus. A roar like the ocean howled in her ears. The plane's engines, or her own pulse?

When she opened her eyes, she saw General holding a gun up to BO Dude's head.

"Captain," he called out in a loud voice, "I'd say you better straighten this plane out right now." He glanced around the cabin with a cocky grin. "As for the rest of you here, I suggest you get out your phones." He spoke in a monotone that gave Kennedy more chills than Scrooge when he faced the Ghost of Christmas Yet to Come.

Once two or three dozen phone cameras were pointed at him, General started his monologue.

"My name is Bradley Strong. Until this morning, I resided at 324 Trenton Street in Detroit, Michigan. I have here as hostages one hundred and seventeen passengers and five crew members of Flight 219 ..."

The speech was interrupted by some kind of metal music screaming from the PA system. Kennedy threw her hands over her ears to dampen the sound.

"Turn that off!" General yelled. He stared at the cabin ceiling, as if the speakers themselves could understand him.

"Once more, this is your captain." He spoke over the sound of the death metal with a hint of amusement in his tone. "I'm sorry for the interruption, but we have a strict nofeeding-the-lunatics policy onboard, which means that we won't allow this cabin to become a soapbox. I'd ask all you sane, reasonable passengers to please put your phones away and ignore empty threats from ..."

"How's this for an empty threat?" General asked in a chilling monotone.

Kennedy had time to shut her eyes and scrunch her body into an even smaller ball before the shot cracked through the pressurized air. She didn't see BO Dude fall or hear the thud his body made when he dropped.

"I hope some of you were recording that." General spoke more quietly now that the horrific music had stopped streaming over the speakers.

She waited for the captain to speak.

Silence.

"What did I tell you earlier?" General shrugged. "All I want is a little respect and cooperation."

"Are you ok?" Ray whispered.

Kennedy tried to nod, but she wasn't sure if her muscles actually worked. For a brief second, she felt an uncontrollable urge to giggle. She imagined the captain flooding the cabin with nitrous oxide, pictured how General would look as he tried to fight it but finally gave into the irresistible urge, like Patrick Stewart playing Scrooge in *A*

Christmas Carol and learning to laugh for the very first time when he woke up on Christmas morning.

Kennedy glanced around the cabin. So many people. She didn't know much about guns, but knew there couldn't be that many bullets, right? What if they all took their chances, all stormed General at once? There might be a few injuries, but nearly everyone was guaranteed to survive. If the plane were full of Vulcans, they would have made the logical decision by now.

She felt another almost irresistible urge to bust her gut laughing when she pictured Leonard Nemoy playing Spock and incapacitating their assailants with his Vulcan death grip. If this were *Star Trek*, the smelly man would have worn a red uniform instead of a Seahawks sweatshirt.

Thinking of the fallen passenger forced stark reality into Kennedy's cerebral cortex. This wasn't a sci-fi show. This wasn't a comedy or staged melodrama. There was no laughing gas. There was nothing humorous at all here.

She trembled even harder, certain now she was about to throw up. She saw a barf bag in Ray's seatback pocket and pointed. "Could you ..."

She didn't get the rest of the question out. Ray moved his foot out of the way, but some of the spray still landed on the leg of his pants. Kennedy wanted to apologize but was too scared to talk, scared that if she drew attention to herself, she'd be the next person General chose to turn into a sacrificial example.

General stepped over the crumpled man's body and addressed the cabin again. "Now that I've got your attention, let's try this one more time. I want you all to get your cell phones out. Now."

Ten seconds later, at least a hundred cell phones were pointed at General, who smiled for the cameras before he began his speech one more time.

CHAPTER 10

"My name is Bradley Strong. I reside at 324 Trenton Street in Detroit, Michigan. For all you law officers listening in, I wouldn't bother sweeping the place if I were you. Everything's scrubbed."

His voice was smooth, confident, as if he'd been born to speak into video cameras at forty thousand feet.

"You might be interested to know that I'm on Flight 219 and have here a hundred and seventeen passengers ..." He glanced down at his feet. "Actually, correct that. I have here a hundred and sixteen passengers and five crew members as my hostages. I'm with my lieutenant, who for the time being shall remain nameless."

He nodded at Hawaiian Shirt and smirked at the cameras. Kennedy wondered how many of the recordings were streaming to a live audience. How long until the news channels picked up the feed? How long until her parents learned where she was? She wished she had her phone with her, not so she could immortalize General's morbid oration but so she could call her mom and dad.

She had slumped down in her seat as far as she could go. She didn't want to see General. Didn't want to think about the dead man at his feet. Ray wasn't recording the video either. "Do you have a phone?" she asked him, trying to figure out how to call her parents without having their number memorized.

"I'm not going to raise publicity for terrorists."

Kennedy wanted to shut her ears. No. He couldn't use words like *terrorist*. Terrorists were men from the Middle East who strapped bombs to their chests and hoped to die with their victims. This was different. A skyjacker. A mentally deranged criminal, but one who wanted to stay alive. Which meant he wanted to keep the plane in the air.

Kennedy thought back to all her dad's stupid crisis training. He hadn't ever mentioned skyjackings, but he'd given her advice about other sorts of hostage situations. The first rule he always drilled into her head was that the typical abductor didn't want to harm his hostages. He needed as much leverage as possible. Well, her dad could spout off rules and generalizations all day long, but that wouldn't change the fact that a man had been shot in the head no less than twenty feet from where she now cowered in fear.

She shouldn't even be here. She should be in the back of the plane with Willow. *Willow.* What if this was it? What if General had a bomb and was planning to bring the whole plane down? What if he was going to shoot hostages one at a time, starting at the back of the plane? Kennedy might never get another chance to talk to Willow again. Never tell her anything about the Lord.

God, I'm so sorry.

What use did her apologies serve? *Man is destined to die once.* She knew that verse from Hebrews. *Destined to die once and after that face judgment.* If something happened to Willow, if she died without knowing Jesus because Kennedy had been too uncomfortable to ask the most important question ...

And after that face judgment. It was Kennedy, not Willow, who deserved to be judged.

Please, God. Help us survive. She'd never thought very highly of folks who made bargains with God when their lives were in danger. Men like Martin Luther who would have never joined the monastery if he hadn't uttered a rash promise seconds after lightning struck the ground beside him. But now here she was, begging God for one last chance. Like Jonah drowning in a storm-tossed ocean, pleading with God for mercy and another chance to preach repentance to the wicked city of Ninevah.

One more chance.

If for no other reason than that Kennedy would never forgive herself if Willow died today. She thought about Gladys Aylward, who was sent to stop a murderous prison uprising with nothing but the power of the Holy Spirit defending her, protecting her. For a moment, she pictured herself standing up with that same degree of faith and conviction, telling General to drop his weapon. It was possible, wasn't it? But her body refused to move, and her only hope was to stay as inconspicuous as possible.

That and pray for Willow's protection.

She's not ready to die yet, Lord. Kennedy had lived her entire Christian life believing in a literal hell. She knew there were some theologians who doubted the existence of an actual lake of fire, but Kennedy had never given their unorthodox hypotheses much credence. But as she looked back, she realized she'd spent the past nineteen years living as if hell weren't a real, physical place where people she knew and loved would spend eternity separated from God if they never learned about his grace and forgiveness. If she actually believed in hell as the Bible described it, was there any way she would have lived with Willow for the past year and a half without even attempting to broach the subject of God's love and mercy?

She's not ready to die yet, Lord, Kennedy repeated, and realized the same went for her. She hadn't seen her parents since last summer. She had so many plans for her life. College graduation. Med school. *Just think of all the things I can do for you if you let me live longer.* There she went again, bargaining with God. If she'd been so concerned about serving him with her life, maybe she should have made better use of the past nineteen years. Maybe she should have focused more on her own spiritual growth so she wasn't terrified to share the gospel with others. Was getting a 4.0 GPA worth seeing her roommate and those around her condemned for all eternity?

It couldn't happen. God loved Willow. Just as much as he loved everyone else on this plane. He couldn't let them all die, not without a chance to hear …

A chance to hear … Could it be that God was giving her that opportunity now? She remembered the story of John Harper, a Christian evangelist from Scotland who found himself crossing the Atlantic Ocean for a speaking engagement at Moody Church. Unfortunately, the ship he was travelling on was none but the Titanic, and when it started to sink, he gave up his own life vest to a passenger who wasn't a Christian, certain that the atheist needed it more than he did.

When the boat capsized, John Harper floundered in the freezing water, swimming from one frantic survivor to another, praying with all of those he met before he himself succumbed to the cold and surrendered his soul to eternity.

Was it possible God was calling Kennedy to be that bold? It couldn't be. John Harper had been an evangelist even before the Titanic's fatal voyage. He had practiced sharing the gospel his whole life. That wasn't Kennedy's spiritual gift, her area of expertise. And so, just like the reluctant prophet Jonah, she begged God to send someone else. Someone like Grandma Lucy. She'd been a missionary and told people about Jesus all the time, including the son of the Afghani man with pneumonia. If God would call anyone to tell the passengers on this flight about the way to salvation, he'd assign the task to Grandma Lucy.

If she was even awake.

Kennedy thought about the man who'd been shot just moments earlier. Had he been a Christian? Would she ever know? And if he died unsaved, was there anything she could have done to change his fate? No. She couldn't handle that sort of liability. She didn't want it. Let her be the one to pray quietly in the background or offer moral support while others went out and shared the gospel. Kennedy couldn't live with the weight of someone's eternal destiny on her conscience. It wasn't her responsibility.

"I suppose some of you are wondering why I'm doing this." General's words snapped her back to reality. To the fact that a madman with a gun was addressing the world via a hundred different recording devices and was about to explain his rationale.

Kennedy silenced the protests of her guilty conscience. She wasn't about to miss General's words.

CHAPTER 11

"My children attend Brown Elementary School," General began.

Kennedy was surprised. She would never have pictured a heartless murderer as the type who would also be a father.

"Unless you're from Michigan, you probably haven't even heard about our little school. That's because the media doesn't care. They don't care that Charles Weston has failed our kids as the district superintendent. Traded in our children's health to save the state a few bucks by building their school on toxic land."

General paused and stared at the cameras. "The soil's got arsenic in it. And not just little bits. We've got numbers. Forty times higher than the safe amount. And that's the level advised for adults, not little five-year-olds eating dirt off the playground," he added. "Want an example of how bad it is? Three construction workers on the new school site got sick within one week on the job. One ended up in the ER.

Breathing problems. Is that the kind of soil you'd want to send your kids to play in?"

The hand that held the gun was shaking. Kennedy wondered if one of the passengers close by him could tackle him while he was focused on his speech. Tackle him without getting killed in the process.

"The site of the new school building, they used to have a pharmacy company on it. Know what the workers dug up? Two underground storage tanks." He wiped his forehead with his fist. "Charles Weston dumped them in secret before anyone could test what was in them. He says it's old ground water, but why's water got to be buried ten feet under? And why'd he order the tanks moved in the middle of the night before anyone could test what was in them?" His voice was as impassioned as Kennedy imagined old-time evangelists like Charles Spurgeon's and Dwight Moody's must have been.

"Now, let me ask you something," General continued. Kennedy couldn't tell if he was talking more to the passengers or to their video cameras. "If you were told that your kids' school was going to be built onto a hazardous waste site, that they'd be exposed to contaminants from the air, the soil, and the water there, what would you do?"

He looked around, and Kennedy watched several passengers shift uncomfortably in their seats under his gaze.

Did he really want an answer?

"What would you do?" he demanded again.

"Take it to the district office." Ray's voice beside Kennedy made her jump. She crouched down, hoping General wouldn't focus any of his attention on her.

"Take it to the district office," he repeated with a menacing grin. "And guess what? That's just what we did. We got a petition, demanded a public meeting. Well, Charles Weston and his stooges set up a meeting all right. At four in the flipping afternoon. Know why? 'Cause he knew the parents would still be at work and wouldn't be able to attend. Do you know how bad things have to be to get eighty parents to show up at four in the afternoon on a work day? And we handed Superintendent Weston our proposal. Merge Brown Elementary with Golden Heights just five miles over. Why not? The building's there. The teachers are there. They even have old trailer classrooms that nobody's used in a decade."

He cleared his throat loudly.

"You know what Weston said to our proposal?" He waited again for an answer before supplying one himself. "Absolutely nothing. Know why? Because he didn't show up. He sent his secretary to read a four-word speech Weston penned himself. *Shut up. Go home.* Of course, he put it more eloquently than that. I'm summarizing."

Kennedy's brain was in full-fledged cognitive dissonance mode. This man who cared about justice for his children couldn't be the same man who'd murdered a crabby Seahawks fan minutes earlier. This father who refused to risk his children's health couldn't be the same terrorist who helped Lieutenant kidnap a girl, disabled an air marshal, and hijacked their plane. A familiar constricting of her lungs. A suffocating, choking feeling she'd worked so hard to avoid all semester.

At least her body understood this was a perfect time to panic.

She bit the inside of her cheek, hoping the pressure might give her something to focus on other than her terror. Her mouth still tasted like vomit. She squeezed her eyes shut, trying to push back the darkness and paralyzing dread that threatened to envelop her. How many times could anxiety take control of you before you lost yourself completely in the fight? How many times could she try to overcome her PTSD only to find herself thrown into a new scenario more terrifying and dangerous than the last? How many times could she pray for healing and fail to find it before her spirit succumbed to depression and despair?

No. She couldn't give in to dark thoughts.

But where else was there to turn?

Her breathing came in shallow spurts. She felt each restrictive inhale like the stinging of killer bees swarming inside her lungs.

God help me, she whispered and wondered why she even bothered. How many times had she prayed before in a crisis? How many times had God left her to flounder, left her to fend for herself in a helpless, hopeless situation? How many injustices had she prayed against, only to find her prayers powerless to confront the degree of evil and devastation that swarmed unchecked around the globe?

Her soul begged God to help her, but her mind knew she was completely alone. God had no reason to listen to her. She was nothing. A college student. She'd never led a single soul to Christ, never gone on a single mission trip. Even as a teenager in China, she'd spent more time reading or shopping for clothes than praying and studying with the North Korean refugees her parents took in as part of their Secret Seminary training.

Her last year and a half at Harvard had been a huge waste of time. What did God care about her GPA? What did he care about her lab results? She'd made academic success her idol, couldn't even get into the habit of attending church every week, and refused to share the gospel with the one person on campus she talked to on a regular basis.

She was a failure as a Christian, especially when she compared herself to her parents' Secret Seminary students or the heroes of faith she'd been reading about in her biographies. God had no reason to save her, no reason to spare her life, no reason to listen to her prayers at all.

Please, God ...

She remembered what Pastor Carl had said during the last sermon of his she'd heard. He talked about God's love for everyone, his unconditional, limitless love. Where was that love when he allowed Hawaiian Shirt to kidnap a helpless girl? Where was that love when he stood by while BO Dude got shot? Where was that love now when every single breath Kennedy took was shallower and more forced than the last?

Kennedy had grown up learning about God's love, but what good had it done her? It hadn't stopped her from getting kidnapped her freshman year. Hadn't shielded her from the horror of police brutality last spring. Hadn't kept her lab partner from contracting an incurable disease. It hadn't even healed her PTSD.

Maybe she should stop fearing the inevitable and be glad she ended up on a doomed plane. Maybe this was God's way of putting her out of her misery so she would stop embarrassing him as she stumbled through her so-called Christian existence.

Please, God. She wanted to barter. Wanted to beg. But she knew it was pointless. God's mind was already made up, wasn't it? Either she would die on this plane or she wouldn't. No degree of pleading or whining would change that. She just wished she could talk to her parents one last time ...

General was still lecturing about the toxic land Weston and the school district had purchased for the new elementary building. Funny. Kennedy thought she'd care more. If she was about to die, it made sense that she'd be curious about her murderer's intentions. But now that she was resigned to her fate, what did it matter? Was getting blown up by a Muslim extremist any different than getting shot point-blank by an angry father from Detroit?

You died either way, right?

A heaviness settled over her, not like the peace she'd sometimes experienced in the midst of a crisis where she knew God was ministering to her, but a joyless acceptance of whatever fate would throw her way. Maybe if she'd been a better believer, God would have more reason to save her. For now, she'd just have to sit tight and wonder if the end would come from a bullet, a bomb, or a forty-thousand-foot drop with a fiery finale. Which would be less painful? And if you ended up dead no matter what, did it matter?

"Before I sign out," General concluded, "I have a message for the district superintendent, good old Charles Weston. If I don't hear from you in five minutes, I'm taking out another hostage. You can find my phone number as well as a full description of the crimes you've committed against the children of Detroit on my personal webpage."

After a longer-than-necessary dramatic pause, General growled to the passengers, "Now turn those cameras off. Countdown's started."

CHAPTER 12

The only thing Kennedy could think about was getting back to her seat. Get to Willow no matter what was about to happen to them. Grab her phone and find a way to call her parents. Was it day or night now in Yanji? Adjusting from one time zone to another had become second-nature to her, but now she couldn't focus on anything.

Did her parents already know what was happening? Had the whole country watched General's tirade? What if none of the cell phones could stream from this altitude? What if he'd given the superintendent an ultimatum that nobody heard? What if this Weston guy never responded? Would General just keep shooting people until he ran out of ammunition?

"How many bullets do you think he has?" she asked Ray.

"Not enough for all of us." His answer was hardly comforting.

She glanced back and tried to spot Willow. General was pacing the aisle and seemed distracted, but his Hawaiianshirted lieutenant who stood vigil over the dead body kept his eyes fixed on the passengers, scowling at each individual in turn.

It wasn't right. She should be with her roommate. With her backpack and her phone. Several of the other passengers were whispering into their cells, probably calling loved ones on the ground.

Kennedy looked at Ray. "At least everyone must know what's happening by now, right?"

Ray frowned. "That's just what he wants."

She didn't know what to say. She didn't know a thing about politics, about hostage negotiations. In her mind, it made sense that the more people who knew about the situation the better. It meant that many more people were working together to find a way to protect everybody on board.

She thought about the family that had gotten off the plane, and she was thankful those children didn't have to experience this kind of terror.

"So you don't think anybody's going to call?" Kennedy asked.

Ray sighed. "All I know is if everyone on this plane refused to play into his little act, he'd have no leverage. That's all these terrorists want. Sensationalism. His only goal's to drive media attention to this school issue, and he'll try anything to do it."

Kennedy didn't answer. She was thinking about Grandma Lucy's grandson and how his story had been replaced with something more noteworthy. Ray was probably right.

"Get a plane full of civilians," he went on, "and you're guaranteed media updates every minute. Everyone's talking about the passengers, the skyjacker, the issues involved, and bam. The story's viral."

He tapped onto his phone's newsfeed and showed her the screen. "See?" He read the headline out loud. "*Home-Grown Terrorism: Flight 219.*" He scrolled a little farther down. "Or here. *Detroit School District's Dirty Soil Secret.* All he had to do was take over one plane, and Brown Elementary School's a household name. If he hadn't already shot a man, half of these news outlets would be hailing him a hero right now."

Kennedy didn't care about the hijacker's cause. Calloused as it sounded, she didn't even care about the school kids in Detroit as much as she cared about getting off this plane. Why hadn't the captain said anything in so long? Was he even with them anymore, or had the plane switched to autopilot? Had something horrible happened to him in the cockpit?

"I want to go back to my seat," she said. "I really should stay with Willow."

"I wouldn't do that if I were you." Ray shook his head. "You don't want to draw attention to yourself …"

"But Willow …"

"… would rather have a living friend than a dead one," he finished for her.

Kennedy bit her lip. Maybe he was right. What would happen if General didn't get his call by the time his five minutes ran out? He'd already proven how easily he could kill. There was absolutely nothing to stop him from doing it again.

A hundred and sixteen passengers. It wasn't terrible odds. Earlier on the flight, she'd been feeling sorry for herself that she wasn't the kind of girl to stand out in a crowd. Maybe that would work out in her favor. What threat did a nineteen-year-old college sophomore pose? As long as she crouched low in her seat, didn't try anything stupid, General would never notice her.

For a fleeting moment, she pictured herself standing up in the cabin, telling all the passengers, including General and Lieutenant, about Jesus. It was crazy. Maybe she was having dark thoughts, but she wasn't suicidal. No, she just had to get through these next couple of hours alive. That's all it would be. A couple hours max. They were already close to Detroit. The plane couldn't stay in the air indefinitely. It would have to come down one way or another. *This too shall pass …*

And then she'd tell Willow about the Lord. That was the bargain she'd make with God. If he got both of them out of this alive, she'd spend the next year if necessary preaching the gospel to Willow every hour of the day.

If they survived.

General was walking up the aisle next to Kennedy when his timer beeped in his pocket. He raised his eyebrows and stared at his phone.

"That's five minutes," he declared. "Time's up."

CHAPTER 13

Nobody talked. Kennedy kept her eyes on the ground as General passed her by. He wore faded Nikes, with the sole of one shoe starting to peel away. She couldn't explain why it struck her as strange. Here he was, ready to kill over a hundred civilians while an entire nation watched, and he was wearing shabby shoes.

Maybe he wasn't so scary after all.

Or maybe that was the cognitive dissonance talking.

He strolled the aisle slowly, his gun swinging low in his hand. Why didn't someone grab it?

"Are you recording?" he asked the man in the Hawaiian shirt. Kennedy wondered what news source his camera fed. Were people watching this in real time? What if he had a bomb? What if the plane exploded? They wouldn't really air that live on network television, would they?

At least while General addressed the camera his focus was diverted from the rest of the passengers on the plane. Five minutes had come and gone, and nobody called.

Kennedy would have never guessed a school zoning issue could lead to terrorism.

No, not terrorism. That was the wrong word. General wasn't a terrorist. He was psychotic. He didn't have any political connections to any other organizations. He was working on his own, just him and Lieutenant who jumped in to kidnap girls or take out air marshals as the need arose. That didn't make General a terrorist. To be a terrorist, he had to have some umbrella organization sending him out, pumping his brain full of propaganda and then sanctioning this suicide mission.

He wasn't a terrorist. He was just insane.

"Mr. Weston," General's voice boomed throughout the otherwise still cabin. "You've had five and a half minutes to respond to my request to talk. You've sat at the negotiating table with your teachers' union. You know how this goes. If I don't stand by my threat, my word means nothing anymore. I just want you to remember, Mr. Weston, that everything that happens from this moment on is your fault."

There was a malicious sort of coyness in his tone that sent pinpricks zinging up and down Kennedy's spine.

"Entirely your fault," he repeated. He marched the aisle slowly, staring at each passenger in turn. His eyes landed on

Kennedy for a brief second, and her blood chilled the same way Scrooge's must have when his door knocker revealed the face of his long-dead partner.

He kept walking. Slowly. Deliberately. All the way to the back of the plane. Not to Willow ...

Kennedy's stomach flipped in her gut as he smiled gallantly at the flight attendant. "Come here, darling."

She hesitated for only a minute and then stepped toward him.

"What's your name?" he asked, his voice purring like a cat's.

"Tracy."

He held her by the arm, positioning her slightly in front of himself. "Tell me, Tracy, do you have children?"

She was shaking. She bit her lip and nodded once.

"How charming," General answered. "How many?"

"Two." Her voice was hardly above a whisper. She squeezed her eyes shut.

General pouted into the camera. "I assume you'd like to see them again, wouldn't you?" He raised the gun toward her temple.

She nodded once more. Her teeth chattered until she clamped down on her jaw. Kennedy saw the strain in the muscles of her neck.

General let out a dramatic sigh. "Mr. Weston, you have two new orphans on your conscience."

The shot deafened Kennedy's ears and reverberated throughout the cabin.

CHAPTER 14

Kennedy hid her face in her arms as General addressed the superintendent of the Detroit School District once more. "You have another five minutes, Mr. Weston. I'm sure you're getting the picture by now. The plane's fully loaded, and I've got all the time in the world. You know how to reach me."

Ray wrapped an arm around Kennedy's shoulder. "It's going to be ok," he whispered. It was a lie but a compassionate one.

She didn't bother replying.

Five minutes. And then the terror would begin anew. Who this time? And how could any of the passengers on board survive this horror? This uncertainty?

Kennedy's teeth chattered. Just like the flight attendant's had before …

Would she ever get that image out of her brain? Could she ever erase the memory of the day? If she survived at all …

A nice trip to Alaska. That's all this was supposed to be.

Her chance to see the northern lights for the first time. Spend a few weeks with Willow, get to know her family, try her first taste of roadkill moose. Why did she have to be on this flight? Why did she have to be so far away from home?

She wanted to call her parents. Wanted to hear her dad's strong, comforting voice. She'd even take the inevitable ten-minute interrogation from her mom about everything from Kennedy's dating life to her personal hygiene habits. Why had she ever left home in the first place?

In the 1800s, missionaries would take months getting from one destination to another. Sometimes they died in the process. Shipwrecks, illnesses at sea were very real dangers these men and women knew about when they set out. For a long time, missionaries to China would pack their belongings in coffins since many of them expected to die on foreign soil.

But that wasn't the world Kennedy had been born into. People traveled across the world every day of the week. Kennedy had probably circumnavigated the globe half a dozen times by now, all without event. Flying was safe. You were more likely to get mauled by a bear than get killed in a plane crash.

What had gone so horrifically wrong?

General still paced the aisles, and Kennedy's body

tensed every time he walked past. How many minutes had already gone by? When would his timer beep again?

She squeezed her eyes shut, hoping to open them and realize she was still in her dorm, waking up from a nightmare. She and Willow would laugh about it, and then they'd walk to the L'Aroma Bakery in Harvard Square and share a quiet breakfast together before Dominic drove them to the airport to enjoy a safe, quiet Christmas break.

When she opened her eyes, General had stopped just a foot or two away from her. She tried to keep her breathing as quiet as possible, which was hard to do on account of the panicked spasms in her lungs.

"That's five minutes," he told his lieutenant. "Let's roll."

Kennedy turned so the cameras wouldn't catch her face. Did her parents know what was happening by now? Were they as freaked out as she was?

General positioned himself in front of Lieutenant's camera. "Mr. Weston, you've had five more minutes to do something about the situation at Brown. I'm a little disappointed I haven't heard from you yet. I wasn't hoping to have to do this, but you've left me with very few options."

General walked toward the front of the plane, and Kennedy's body relaxed just a little the farther away from her he got.

"Mr. Weston, you're a family man. You have kids of your own. Kids you would hate to see hurt, so I know you can empathize with my situation here." He grabbed Selena, the girl who'd been kidnapped, and pulled her up from her first-class seat. "Say hello to Papa," he told her.

Selena's voice trembled. "Daddy?"

General grimaced. "Daddy?" he repeated in a grating falsetto and chuckled into the camera. "I expect I'll be hearing from you soon. As a show of good will, you've got two extra minutes."

His cell phone rang less than ten seconds later. He grinned and pulled it out of his pocket slowly and deliberately before tapping a button.

"Hello, you're on speaker phone."

"Great, that's great. You should know how much I appreciate …"

"Who's this?" General's face darkened into an ugly scowl. "I want to talk to Charles Weston."

"I know. Believe me, I understand your concerns." The voice was smooth. Silky even in its digitized form.

"Who are you?" General demanded again.

"This is Franklin, but all my friends call me Frank. Come to think of it, you had a brother named Frank, didn't you, Bradley?"

"I don't care who you are," General snarled. "I didn't ask to talk to some negotiator shrink. If I don't get Charles Weston on the phone in five seconds, his daughter bites it."

Selena's eyes were wide, but she didn't tremble or make any noise.

"I can only guess how tense things are up there, Bradley," the buttery voice said. "Listen, I've got Mr. Weston on the way right now to chat with you about his daughter, and while we wait for him, how about you take me off speaker phone and we have a little man-to-man chat, just you and me in private?"

General was so tense, it looked as if his eyes might burst out of his skull without warning. "You're staying on speaker."

"Hey, that's cool," Frank went on, "but I want to ask you something. I know you've had some trouble up there. Is there anything you need? Are any of the passengers hurt? We've got a doctor down here. He can talk you through any first aid you might require."

"Just shut up and get me Weston," General snarled.

There was a long pause before the voice came back. "Ok, I just heard from your man. He says he's real concerned for his daughter and wants to patch up this little misunderstanding you two have as soon as possible."

"Great. Put him on the phone."

"Yeah, that's not feasible right at this moment, but I'll tell you what we can …"

"No," General interrupted, "I'll tell you what. You get Weston on the phone with me in three more minutes, or I kill his daughter."

Selena didn't cringe. Kennedy wondered if she knew what was going on or if her brain had shut down completely because of all the trauma.

Frank's voice on the other line was just as even and calm. "Hmm, I don't think you want to do that. Sounds to me like Selena's your biggest bargaining chip right now, wouldn't you say? Let's think about another way to settle these differences you two men are experiencing or …"

"Fine," General spat. "Three minutes to talk to Weston, or another hostage dies." He punched his phone off so hard Kennedy would have been surprised if his screen survived the ordeal.

"Set the timer," General snapped at Lieutenant. "Three more minutes."

The entire cabin was silent except for the droning of the engines. A numbness akin to Selena's psychological coma seemed to have settled into the collective psyche of the passengers. Nobody was crying. Nobody was carrying on whispered conversations. Most, like Kennedy, stared blankly ahead.

Waiting.

Three more minutes. Kennedy found herself thinking about Einstein's theory of relativity. Technically, since they were on an airplane, wouldn't three minutes up here pass more slowly than on the ground? Too bad the difference was miniscule. If this were a sci-fi book, maybe they could take advantage of the time distortion, but this wasn't speculative fiction, and the grating squeal from Lieutenant's timer pounded in Kennedy's brain like a siren when it went off.

"Time's up." General started his slow march to the back of the plane.

Past Kennedy and Ray. Past the rows of passengers who were too tired or shocked to even cringe.

All the way to the back of the cabin.

No. Kennedy's heart screamed the word. *No. No. No.* Was God listening? Could he hear?

General stopped when he reached the last aisle. Kennedy couldn't watch. Why didn't her body turn away? Why didn't her eyes close?

No.

It couldn't be happening. It wasn't happening. There was no way to wrap her mind around any of this. Her brain was begging her for answers, pleading with her to come up with some sort of mental contortion that could explain away this sort of terror, this sort of unfathomable reality. Every joule of energy was focused on that one word. That one thought. That one prayer.

No.

"Stand up."

This wasn't real. This wasn't true. But it was. She couldn't deny it. Couldn't twist reality any other way as General yanked Willow to her feet by a clump of her striking blue hair.

CHAPTER 15

Kennedy was about to spring out from her seat, but Ray held her back.

"There's nothing you can do," he hissed in her ear.

That wasn't true either. He was lying. Her eyes were lying, too. That wasn't Willow who stood with her hands covering her face. That wasn't Willow lifting up one soft request for her life. That wasn't Willow cowering just a foot away from General's gun.

General waited while Lieutenant maneuvered himself to get the best camera angle. Willow had ceased her begging but was looking around the cabin wildly.

Looking for Kennedy?

Jesus saves! She should scream it now. Scream it as loudly as possible. Shout out the four steps to salvation, the sinner's prayer, anything. Give Willow some sort of hope that she could hold onto. Give her that chance to receive God's gift of salvation. How many opportunities had Kennedy already missed? How many times could she have broached the subject in their cramped dorm room? What kind of fellowship might they have shared together?

And now, she was too late.

"Mr. Weston, I'd like you to meet a young friend of mine." General smiled as Willow tried to shrink into the wall to get away from him.

Just tell her, something burning inside Kennedy's soul shouted. *Tell her now.* But the words wouldn't come. Ray was holding onto her shoulder, whether to offer some sort of protection or to keep her from joining her roommate in her death.

"She doesn't want to die, and if you must know the truth, I don't want to kill her. But a word is a man's bond, isn't that right, Mr. Weston?" General raised up the corner of his lip in a half smirk.

Take me instead. The thought came to her in an instant, and her brain flashed with an image John Harper, the preacher on the capsizing Titanic who gave away his own life jacket because he couldn't stand the thought of a man dying without having the chance to know Christ.

Take me instead. Why wouldn't her mouth work? Why wouldn't her body move? Why wouldn't Ray let her go?

"Anyway, for those of you watching this drama unfold, I want you to remember one name. Charles Weston. Detroit

School District superintendent. If it weren't for Charles Weston, I wouldn't have to send my children to a schoolyard that's put grown men in the hospital. And if it weren't for Charles Weston, I wouldn't have to shoot this rather pretty passenger."

"You'll do no such thing, young man."

Kennedy gaped at the old woman who addressed General with so much boldness and conviction.

He let out a gruff laugh. "You, granny? What are you going to do?"

Grandma Lucy was out of her seat, the cowboy bandana still in her hand. "Do?" she asked. "I'm going to save this young woman's life."

Kennedy's heart was racing. She was going to throw up again. Any minute now. She couldn't hold it down much longer.

Grandma Lucy stepped next to Willow, who flung her arms around her like a preschooler clutching at her mother's skirt.

"I've given my word," General explained. "It's time for me to kill a hostage."

Grandma Lucy swept Willow behind her. "Then you'll kill a hostage whose soul is ready to enter paradise, and you'll leave this poor child out of it." She sucked in her breath, stuck out her chest, and waited.

The air in the cabin changed. Denser now. Was anybody on board still breathing?

General glanced once at Lieutenant and then shrugged. "A hostage is a hostage." He held out his gun until the barrel was only a foot away from Grandma Lucy's forehead.

She didn't flinch. "Before you kill me, there's something I'd like to tell you. Something your audience might be interested in hearing."

He raised an eyebrow impatiently. "Yeah? What's that?"

She tilted up her chin. "That Jesus Christ is the risen Savior of the world. He is my shepherd, my redeemer, my healer, and my coming king. If you kill me, my soul will leave this broken jar of clay and enter into the presence of God."

"Great," General muttered. "So I guess I'm doing you a favor."

"Yes, you are." Grandma Lucy took a step closer to him, pressing Willow several paces behind her with a protective sweep of her hand. "And since you're doing me such a great honor, I want to return the favor."

"How you expect to do that?"

Grandma Lucy's voice was perfectly steady. "I'd like to pray for you."

He scoffed.

"I'm volunteering to die for your cause. In a way, I'll be your first martyr, isn't that right? So you let me pray for you, and then I promise not to interfere when you pull that trigger. In fact, by killing me, you'll be winning yourself lots of added publicity. Know why? My grandson made a documentary about Brown Elementary School last fall. Put four months of his own time and his own money into it."

General shuffled from one foot to another. "I never heard about a documentary."

"It never aired," Grandma Lucy told him. "But I guarantee that if you kill me, everyone will be clamoring to watch my grandson's show. The public will be on your side. You'll be sure to get justice. Now, will you let me pray for you?"

He stared at Lieutenant once more before finally grumbling, "Fine. But keep it short."

Grandma Lucy had already closed her eyes and raised her hands toward heaven. "Father God, sweet Savior, my friend, this is a man who is hurting. This is a man who has a deep desire to see justice. This is a father who cares for his children, who hates the thought of seeing them come to harm due to man's ignorance and greed. Give rest to his soul, Father God. Comfort him. Strip him free of the burdens he carries, his anger, his rage, his insecurities. Settle his spirit, Lord, so that he can find true rest in you, the giver of life. The author of peace. The comfort of our souls. Teach him, Holy Spirit, that there is no other name under heaven by which he can be saved than the sweet name of Jesus Christ, the Lamb of God who takes away the sins of the world. Show him that his guilt will be washed clean, whiter than snow, if he confesses his sins, if he believes that you died for him, that you took the penalty for his transgressions upon your bloody shoulders when you hung on that beautiful, glorious cross. Show him, Jesus, that you are the way, the truth, and the life, that no one can come to the Father except through you. Give him a burning desire to know you, Lord, so that he can say like the Apostle Paul that *Christ came into the world to save sinners, of whom I was the worst*. Without you, sweet and merciful Jesus, we are all wretched. Without you, we are sinful, unable to do anything good. But because of the blood that you shed …"

"That's enough!" General roared.

Kennedy cowered involuntarily in her seat.

General raised his gun once more. His whole body was shaking. "I said that's enough," he snarled again, even though Grandma Lucy stood calmly and hadn't said a word.

Kennedy tensed her muscles. Braced herself for the

upcoming explosion. Squinted her eyes so they'd be ready to close that much faster as soon as he pulled the trigger.

"Go ahead, young man," Grandma Lucy urged. "I've been ready to meet my Jesus for over fifty years."

Kennedy squeezed her eyes shut and covered her ears with her hands.

CHAPTER 16

Click.

Kennedy pried one eye half open. Had she heard right?

Click.

No louder than a retractable pen collapsing on itself. General stared at his gun in stunned rage.

Grandma Lucy opened her eyes and smiled at him sweetly. "I should have mentioned one more thing. God promised me in the book of Isaiah chapter 54 that no weapon forged against me would prevail."

General stared stupefied.

Ray sprung out of his seat. "His gun doesn't work!"

Three other men jumped up at the same time. Two tackled the fat lieutenant in his Hawaiian shirt from behind, sweeping his legs out from under him and letting his own body weight do the rest. Ray and someone in a dark suit confronted General head on, both working to twist the gun out of his hold. Ray finally succeeded and slid out the cartridge, tossing it up the aisle toward Kennedy. The second man doubled over when

General punched him in the gut, but by then a few other passengers and the unbound air marshal had joined in the fray. Kennedy could only see a blur of colors, hear the cacophonous sounds of *oofs* and curses and flailing limbs. Breath whooshed back into her lungs, choppy and uncertain at first like a child just learning to toddle. Would it ever end?

She tried to focus on Ray to make sure he was ok, but she could never keep her eyes on him for long. Her brain couldn't follow the disjointed movements of the skirmish, didn't dare hope the passengers would succeed.

Were the cameras still rolling? Did the viewers see what was happening?

"We got them!" The male flight attendant shouted. "We have both men subdued."

The cabin filled with air again. Relief. Release. Kennedy pried her fingers loose from her seatbelt. So it was really over. Their salvation had come in by way of a grandmother with the boldness of an advancing army and the miracle of a misfired weapon.

"You're all dead!" General shouted as the air marshal dragged him to the back of the cabin. "Nobody's getting off this plane alive!"

The PA system came on. "Folks, this is your captain speaking, and I just want to say thank you to everyone back there who kicked some terrorist butt."

Nervous laughter and subdued applause began to melt away the fear that had frozen like armor around Kennedy's psyche. She allowed herself a smile, noted the strange sensation of her facial muscles as it spread across her face.

A woman with shocking blue hair, glossy as a marble, threw herself into the seat by Kennedy and wrapped her arms around her. "We're safe."

"You're all dead!" General shouted from the back of the plane.

A sob rose from Kennedy's chest and lodged itself in her throat.

Willow shook her gently by the shoulders. "It's ok now."

Terror, fear, guilt, and shock took over Kennedy's entire body. She hadn't realized how much energy it had taken just to keep them all contained. Now they came bursting out of her core with the explosive energy of a nuclear detonation.

Willow didn't seem surprised by the tears that coursed down Kennedy's cheeks. She didn't laugh at her. Didn't tease. Just gave her another hug, whispering those beautiful words over and over again like a prayer of thanksgiving.

"We're safe."

CHAPTER 17

The moments that followed General's failure felt more surreal than any dream Kennedy could remember. While General and his lieutenant sat bound in the back of the plane, the passengers slowly began to talk again. Move around again. Breathe again. The two dead bodies were covered with blankets and moved out of the aisles. Out of sight. Could Kennedy ever forget? What had she known about Tracy? A mother of two. Frazzled at times, perhaps, but she did her job well. What would her friends say about the kind of person she was off hours? Her husband or any other loved ones she'd left behind?

She squeezed her eyes shut. Thank God they were so close to Detroit. She had to wrangle her thoughts. Take them captive. Avoid thinking about Tracy and the other murdered passenger. At least until she landed on solid ground. Not until she achieved the psychological security that would come from getting off this plane.

"You're all dead!" General shouted before the air

marshal punched him in the face.

Kennedy, Willow, and Ray were scrunched up together in the row where his math tests had been strewn across the aisle. The three of them struggled together to make sense of his mess.

"Folks," the captain said, "I'm sure we're all ready to get off this aircraft. I'm happy to report that we're beginning our descent now to Detroit. I imagine the deboarding process will be a little bit unorthodox, and we've got a whole army of first responders ready to assist in any way they can. Please buckle up and prepare for a safe and uneventful landing."

Kennedy still had a hard time believing it was over. As if a nightmare that ghastly couldn't end so simply. Were they really about to touch down in Detroit? She didn't care if it took them a week to get to Anchorage. For now, she was just ready to have her feet connected to the solid earth.

Everything had happened so fast. The hijacking, the countdowns, the scrimmage that overcame their would-be killers. Kennedy had the feeling it would take her all of Christmas break and half of spring semester just to process everything that happened, and then another few years of prayer and counseling to actually move past it.

The skyjackers had been thwarted. That's what mattered. Willow laughed at something Ray said, but Kennedy could only hear their tentatively joyful conversation as though through a fog.

Her roommate had almost died. Everyone had been close to death, but Willow had been a foot away from a loaded gun. If it hadn't been for Grandma Lucy ...

"Where are you going?" Willow asked when Kennedy got up from her seat.

"I think the captain wants everyone to stay buckled," Ray told her.

Kennedy wasn't listening. She made her way to the back of the plane, where Grandma Lucy sat in the corner, hunched over her Bible. She looked up with a smile before Kennedy sat down.

"I was hoping for a chance to chat with you." She moved her purse so Kennedy could settle in beside her. "I've been reading. Here in Isaiah." She pointed to some verses in her large print Bible.

Lift up your eyes to the heavens, look at the earth beneath, Kennedy read to herself, nodding as if she fully understood whatever spiritual mysteries Grandma Lucy expected her to find.

"Keep going," she said. "Read it out loud."

Kennedy took in a breath. "*The heavens will vanish like smoke, the earth will wear out like a garment and its inhabitants die like flies. But my salvation will last forever, my righteousness will never fail.*" Well, she had certainly seen God's salvation today, seen it in a way she would never forget. But something had been bothering her ever since it happened. Something she had to know now.

She looked up from the book. "Were you sure the gun wouldn't fire?"

Grandma Lucy slipped her spectacles back up her nose. "No. I wasn't. But I had a peace." She stared at Kennedy pointedly. "Did you?"

"Know about the gun?" she asked.

Grandma Lucy shook her head. "No. Did you have that peace?"

Kennedy thought back to the darkness, the overwhelming despair, the guilt she'd experienced when Willow stood at the end of the barrel. She stared at her lap. "No. I didn't."

"That's nothing to be ashamed of." Grandma Lucy tilted up her chin. "God works in each of us in different ways. For me, God used our little excitement today to teach me that I'm ready to go home. I've had my share of health issues lately. Twice now I've surprised the doctors by leaving the hospital in my own car and not in a hearse. And both of those times, I struggled. Told God he couldn't take me home yet.

I still had to see my grandson saved. I still have to be here to pray for him through whatever trials God uses to bring him to salvation."

She stared past Kennedy's shoulder with a faraway look in her eye.

"When I stared at that gun, though, that's when I knew. The battle for Ian's soul, the battle I've been fighting restlessly for years now, that battle was never mine to begin with. That battle belongs to the Lord and no one else. If he wants me to stay put and pray for my grandson, love him, witness to him, then bless the Lord, oh my soul, because I'm longing to wrap my arms around him the day he finally gives his life over to Christ. But if God calls me to heaven first, then I figure I'll just go on praying for Ian there. I don't see why I can't. That was what God wanted to teach me today. I wonder what lesson he had in store for you."

Kennedy fixed her eyes on the open Bible before her. *Hear me, you who know what is right, you people who have taken my instruction to heart: Do not fear the reproach of mere mortals or be terrified by their insults.*

She took a breath and tried to collect her thoughts. "I think the worst part about today was knowing that if Willow died and went to hell, I'd have to live wondering if I could have done something. If it was my fault that she never learned about the gospel." She shook her head. "I can't believe all the excuses I made. How scared I was of looking dumb or being called judgmental."

Kennedy was ashamed to admit her shortcomings to someone so bold and obedient, but Grandma Lucy just smiled and took Kennedy's hand in hers. "Peter was scared too, remember? But then the Holy Spirit came down at Pentecost, came and settled on him, and the very first time he opened his mouth to preach, the Bible says three thousand new believers were added to their number that day. He wasn't anything more than a simple fisherman with a very good habit of saying the wrong thing at the wrong time, and that's how God used him. So just imagine what he can do with you."

Kennedy sighed. "I'm not sure I'll ever find that kind of power or boldness."

"That's because you're still relying on your own strength. Trust me. I lived my life that way for decades. It wasn't until I followed God's call to Afghanistan that I finally learned what it was to be filled with the Holy Spirit, to surrender not just my eternal life to him, but my day-to-day life as well. Every hour, every minute submitted to him. *What do you want me to do today, Jesus? Who do you want me to tell about you?* That's what I'd ask him. He gave me small assignments at first. Maybe he told me to share a little bit of my lunch with a woman on the streets. And I did that, and then the next time he told me something, it would be a little more out of my comfort zone, like maybe he wanted me to invite two prostitutes into my home and give them a place to sleep. And each time I obeyed, I found a deeper sense of peace. It wasn't that God needed me to reach out to these people. He could have used anybody. But he was inviting me to join him in his work. I stopped looking at it as the relationship between a master and a servant and started to think of it as the partnership between two good friends, both working together for the same goal. He stretched me so much overseas. Taught me what it means to live by the Spirit. I know you're born again, but have you surrendered your life to the Spirit?"

She gazed at Kennedy so pointedly Kennedy stared at her hands in her lap. "I'm not really sure. I think so. I mean, I'm doing my best to read the Bible each day. Remembering to pray."

Grandma Lucy smiled gently. "Let me tell you a story. I got married over fifty years ago. My husband isn't with me anymore, but when we were on our honeymoon, do you think we had to schedule time to spend together?"

Kennedy couldn't figure out what point she was trying to make. "No."

"Of course not. Now, I can tell you there were times in our marriage where we did have to make a conscious effort to connect with each other, but for the most part, we spent time together because we wanted to. Do you see the difference?" she asked and went on without waiting for an answer. "You probably grew up hearing your Sunday school teachers and pastors telling you that to grow in your walk with the Lord, you need to read your Bible and pray every day. Am I right?"

Kennedy nodded.

"And that's true. Without prayer and Scripture, we're not going to mature. But we think of the spiritual disciplines, things like prayer and Bible study, as the definition of spiritual maturity, not the means to grow closer to Jesus. Do you see the difference?"

"I guess so," Kennedy answered even though Grandma Lucy's words didn't seem to connect with her brain in any meaningful way.

Grandma Lucy smiled softly. "I just want you to know that God has so much to offer you. Peace and joy and the riches of his presence. But we get so distracted. We think that if we check morning devotions off our to-do list, we've done everything God expects us to do for the day. It's human nature. I'm not picking on you personally. That's just the way we're programmed. But the Christian walk isn't about a to-do list. Tell me something. If you set aside three hours every single day to study the Bible, do you think you would grow in your faith?"

"Yeah," Kennedy replied tentatively, "but I don't have time to ..."

"I didn't ask about time," Grandma Lucy interrupted. "I just asked if you think it would change your everyday life."

"I'm sure it would."

Grandma Lucy leveled her gaze. "Why?"

"Why?" Kennedy repeated. "Because it's ... Because when you ..."

A smile broke through Grandma Lucy's wrinkled face. "Because we all think that the more time we spend with God, the holier we become, right?"

Kennedy was confused. "Yeah, but isn't that the way it works?"

Another soft smile. "Let me tell you something else. When I first got married, my husband and I both had full-time jobs. I was in real estate at the time. My husband was a teacher. I was busy in the evenings. He left for school at six in the morning. Sometimes we'd go a full week without sitting down for a single meal together. Tell me something. Can you grow close to your spouse with a schedule like that?"

Kennedy frowned. "I guess not."

Grandma Lucy wagged her finger playfully. "You'd think so, right? But actually, that was one of the most intimate times in our relationship. We were so busy we knew we had to put in the extra effort to connect with each other. We'd write letters to each other back and forth in a diary. He'd come home from work and leave me a note while I was out showing houses. In the morning when I woke up, before I started my day's paperwork I'd fill page after page of ridiculous, sappy mush for him to read when he came home in the afternoon."

"Oh." Kennedy had no idea what any of this had to do with her own personal walk with Christ. Maybe Grandma Lucy was just rambling and had lost her original thought.

"Years later when the kids were grown, my husband lost his teaching job and decided to drive trucks. We sold the house, everything. For twelve months, we ate at rest stops, slept in little pullouts, and traveled the country together. Every waking minute, there he was. And want me to tell you something? It tore our marriage apart. By the end of the third month, we couldn't stand each other. The day he delivered his last load was the day I filed for divorce. I'm not saying it was the right thing for me to do. I'm not pretending to be proud of my decision, but that season is what ultimately destroyed us."

By now, Kennedy didn't know what point she was trying to make. Apparently, Grandma Lucy didn't either. She pouted and glanced around the cabin as if looking for some sort of cue card.

"It was when I left my husband that I realized just how terrible I was at being a Christian on my own. I was a disciplined believer, prayed out of a check list and read three or four chapters from the Bible every single night without fail. But that didn't mean I was surrendered to God the other twenty-three and a half hours of the day. Do you know what the Bible says Christian maturity looks like?" She raced ahead without letting Kennedy respond. "The Bible says they'll know we are Christians by our love. Plain and simple. Not how complicated our prayer list is. Not how many times we've read the Bible cover to cover or how long we spend studying it each day. I'll tell you what. There are some deplorable people who I'm sure have read the Bible more than I have and use it to destroy others."

She shook her head. "If we don't have love for each other, what good is all the Bible studying or all the devotional time in the world? What's all that learning doing for us if we're not allowing God's Word to change us? Transform us?"

"Not much, I guess." Kennedy still couldn't tell if she was being reprimanded like a naughty pupil or inspired like a boxer about to jump into the ring.

"And that's where the Holy Spirit comes in." Grandma Lucy's eyes lit, and she nodded sagely, apparently glad to have discovered her train of thought once more. "He's there, waiting for you to fully surrender, waiting for you to invite him to take full control of your life." She stared pointedly at Kennedy. "You strike me as a competent, capable young woman. You're smart, you got yourself into Harvard, you're doing well in your studies. But are you relying on God each and every day? Are you making him the focus of your life? Are you studying to be pleasing to him, or are you studying because you get a thrill from that sense of achievement? When you think about becoming a doctor, is it so you can fulfill the call God has on your life, or is it so you can prove to yourself that you can succeed?"

Kennedy bit her lip. Thankfully, she didn't have to wait long for Grandma Lucy to fill in the uncomfortable silence.

"God has amazing plans for you, but until you learn to surrender to him, until you fall on your knees and beg the Holy Spirit to guide you in every decision you make, you'll always feel like there's something missing." She patted Kennedy's hand. "It's a lot to think about. But when I look at you, I see someone who has so much potential, someone who could do so much to advance the kingdom of God. That's the call you have on your life. To shine his light in a way that everyone around you will recognize the truth of the gospel." She smiled. "And I think you and I both know that can start with your roommate whenever you're ready."

Kennedy had known those words were coming even before Grandma Lucy spoke them. "I'm not sure I'll ever be ready."

Grandma Lucy's eyes crinkled softly. "Here's what Paul says to the Corinthians. He says, *I tell you, now is the time of God's favor, now is the day of salvation.* That pressure you're experiencing, that prompting in your heart that you felt when you saw Willow about to get shot, that's the Holy Spirit. He saved your roommate from death. He didn't have to. He's given both of you a second chance. I suggest you don't waste this one."

Kennedy nodded. Grandma Lucy was right. She hadn't said anything Kennedy didn't already know, but somehow it felt different hearing it from her.

"I just wish I had that kind of boldness," she admitted.

"We can pray for that right now," Grandma Lucy offered and raised one hand heavenward. "Father God, precious Jesus ..."

Her prayer was interrupted by a high-pitched wail coming from the wall directly behind her seat. Kennedy crouched down and covered her ears.

From his confinement behind her, General let out a hair-raising laugh. "Didn't I say you were all about to die?"

CHAPTER 18

"What's going on?" Kennedy asked the flight attendant who rushed past her.

"Smoke alarm," he shouted and pulled a fire extinguisher out from a cabinet.

"Don't waste your time," General chuckled. "It's too late for any of you now."

The flight attendant gave him a half-hearted kick and then flung the bathroom door open. Thick, black smoke poured out from the lavatory. Kennedy's eyes stung, and her lungs were momentarily paralyzed.

"Get to the front of the cabin." The flight attendant waved them away. Kennedy reached across the aisle for her backpack.

"What about me?" General asked, fear lacing his words for the first time.

"You shut up."

Another low chuckle. "I deserved that, I suppose. Just remember, I did this for my kids."

The flight attendant didn't respond. Kennedy grabbed Grandma Lucy's hand, and the two stumbled down the aisle.

"Fire!" As soon as word got out in the cabin, half the passengers jumped out of their seats and lurched forward as one chaotic, undulating mass.

Thick, black smoke choked the air as everyone tried to scramble forward at once.

"Stay calm!" Grandma Lucy shouted behind Kennedy, but even her authoritative voice couldn't carry over the din of the panicked passengers.

"Folks," the captain announced over the PA, "I understand there's a situation in the back, and we're doing what we can to touch down as soon as possible. When we land, we've got to exit the aircraft in a calm and orderly manner. It's going to be a fast descent, so I need you all to get yourselves buckled in."

He may as well have been speaking to himself. Even if Kennedy wanted to move, she was pressed on all sides by people struggling to surge ahead.

"He's trying to kill us!" a woman shouted.

"I can't see anything!"

Grandma Lucy put her hand on Kennedy's shoulder and used it for balance as she stood on one of the empty aisle seats. "Listen, all of you!" she hollered, and the din diminished slightly. "The captain is getting us on the ground. We'll land in just a few minutes and then we'll get off this plane. Right now, there will be more injuries if we all scramble ahead like this. So grab a seat, buckle up, and if you haven't made peace with God yet, I suggest you ask him to forgive your sins in the name of Jesus."

"We're going to die!" someone shrieked. Even if Kennedy could find an empty seat, there were too many bodies pushing against her. The smoke was so thick she couldn't see Grandma Lucy standing on the chair. Had she fallen? Would she see her alive again? She wanted to duck down, knew the air would be cleaner the lower she got, but with the crowd this frantic, if she ended up on the ground there was no way she'd get up again.

The smoke stung her eyes. Kennedy was completely blind now. Her sinuses burned, and she pictured black, sticky tar caking to the epithelial lining of her respiratory tract.

God, help me.

Someone elbowed her in the face. She stumbled back, but a mass of passengers pressed against her from behind. Grabbing her hair, trying to propel themselves forward.

A scream. Not of fear, but of pain. Someone was hurt. Kennedy shot her hands out, trying to regain her bearings. The sea of people had carried her so far she had no idea where she was or if the emergency exits were in front of her or behind. She pried her eyes open, but the smoke was too thick to see anything.

"Let go!"

"Get off!"

"Help!"

The screams were as haunting and terrifying as anything Dante could have dreamed up in his *Inferno*, and for a time Kennedy's mind could only focus on one coherent thought: *This is what hell must be like.*

"I can't breathe," gasped a woman next to her. Kennedy tried to reach out to find her, but as soon as she repositioned her arm someone elbowed her in the gut.

In the midst of the chaos, passengers shouted for one another, calling their loved ones by name.

"Where are you?"

"I can't see you."

"Are you ok?"

Kennedy had to conserve what air was left around her. She was already dizzy. Was that from the fear or the lack of oxygen? If she fainted, if she lost her footing for a moment …

Someone scratched at her face. "Let me through!" A passenger tried to climb up Kennedy's back. She struggled to shove him off.

God, don't let me fall.

Where was Willow? Was she safe? Would she make it? Would any of them survive?

General's voice ran unchecked through her brain. *You're all dead.* He had planned everything. This was his end game.

God, I don't want to die.

Where was Willow?

The passengers pressed ahead, like a legion of lemmings with only one collective thought. With the plane still in the air, Kennedy could only guess where they expected to end up.

Willow. She had to get to her. God had given them a second chance. Grandma Lucy had said the same thing. Would God save her roommate from the gunman only to have her perish in a fire?

"Willow?" She tried to call out, but she couldn't take in enough air to give her voice any volume. "Willow?"

She had to be somewhere, but where?

Dear Lord, show me where she is, and I'll do anything. I'll say anything. Just let her be ok and get us both out of this alive. Please.

Back. Somehow she knew she had to go back. But how could she with all the passengers pressing against her from behind? And why would she want to go where the smoke was the thickest?

God, are you sure?

The impression was there just the same. She had to find her way out of this maddening throng.

She didn't care about the bruises she'd sustain from being prodded and pushed from so many sides. She didn't worry about the germs she was contracting by pressing herself against so many strangers. *God, make a way for me.* She envisioned him parting the bodies around her like he did for Moses at the Red Sea, but that's not what happened. Still, she eventually managed to shove her way to the outskirts of the frantic throng. Safe from the crowd, she dropped to her hands and knees, as much from exhaustion as from a desire to find breathable air.

"Willow?" She was somewhere nearby. Kennedy knew it. Or was that wishful thinking coupled with smoke-induced delirium?

"Willow?"

"Yeah." The voice was frail. Faint. Accompanied by a small cough.

"Where are you?"

"Over here." It was like playing Marco Polo inside a cloud of tear gas.

Kennedy reached ahead with her hand until it clenched a warm, sweaty palm. She could hardly speak, from relief as well as smoke exhaustion. "Are you ok?"

"I can't move."

Colorful spirals fired through Kennedy's optical nerve. She would black out any minute if she didn't get more oxygen.

"My necklace," Willow explained. "I fell, and it's stuck against something. I can't get it loose."

Kennedy probed with her hands until she felt the leather string that held Willow's travel size air purifier. It was hooked to the bottom of the seat and twisted so there wasn't room to slip it over her head.

"It's going to be ok," Kennedy promised, wondering if her last words to Willow would prove to be a lie. She fumbled with blind, clumsy fingers, but every time she tried to free the string, it wound up tighter around Willow's throat.

"We need to cut it." Kennedy would have tried her teeth, but she couldn't pull on it without choking her friend. "God, we need to cut it." She sounded like Grandma Lucy praying out loud like that, but she was well past the point of caring what Willow thought of her faith. She swept her hands around on the floor until she felt a purse beneath one of the seats. Her fingers trembled as she unfastened the clasp. All she needed was a pair of scissors. A nail file. Anything. Why couldn't the passenger have carried a Swiss army knife in her purse?

Stupid TSA regulations.

"I'll have to pull it," Kennedy told her, wincing when she thought about how hard she'd have to yank to get the necklace to break free.

"I don't care. Just get it off."

Kennedy's breaths came out in worried, choked sobs. She couldn't do this. She wasn't strong enough. What if the strap cut into Willow's skin before the necklace gave way? What if she choked her friend to death?

"Just get it off," Willow begged.

Kennedy could feel the heat from the back of the cabin. She didn't have the lung capacity to let out the cry that welled up from her throat. *God, please.* She whispered a silent prayer and yanked with all her might. Willow's head jerked forward and banged Kennedy's knee, but the strap itself held fast.

"I'm sorry," Kennedy squealed.

"Just get it off."

Kennedy braced herself and pressed one hand against Willow's head to keep it still this time. *Ok, God. You performed miracles in the Bible. You performed miracles in the lives of so many missionaries. It's time for a miracle now.* She thought about Grandma Lucy's boldness. Could she conjure up that degree of faith? "In the name of Jesus," she whispered to the necklace, "I command you to break free."

Another yank, so hard Kennedy grunted from exertion.

Nothing. The leather held fast just like the last time, except now Willow didn't respond at all. Had she blacked out? Was she ...

Kennedy leaned down, and her own purifier swung and hit Willow in the face. She grabbed the device to throw it over her shoulder when she felt it. The leather was tied in the back. She ran her hands along Willow's strap until she felt the bulky knot.

"I've got it now," she assured her, but Willow still didn't respond.

God, you can't let her die. You need to give me just one more chance. I won't chicken out again, I promise. Please?

Kennedy slid the leather out of its knot. Her friend was free, but Kennedy couldn't rejoice.

Willow's body lay perfectly limp.

CHAPTER 19

Kennedy planted her fingers against the small dent in Willow's neck. *Please let there be a pulse. Please let there be a pulse.*

There it was. Slow and weak, but at least Willow was still alive. Kennedy leaned down, throwing off her own necklace after the purifier hit Willow in the face again. "You're going to be ok." Tears streamed down her cheeks and dripped onto Willow's body as the plane lurched, flinging Kennedy to one side and then the other. The howl of wind roared through her ears. The cabin floor jostled violently.

From the window Kennedy made out the vague flashing lights of an ambulance.

"We've landed!"

"Out of my way!"

"Watch it!"

Shouting from the front of the plane. Cries of triumph.

Kennedy held onto Willow. In a few minutes, this would all be over.

"Hang on," she pleaded.

"Step aside!"

"Let the paramedics on board."

Kennedy wrapped her arms around Willow and cradled her head in her lap. "Just hang on." It was silly of her, really. Willow couldn't hear a thing, could she?

God, you promised me a second chance. What if this was it? What if Willow was slipping into a coma, a coma she would never wake from? Hadn't Kennedy promised God to share the gospel with her roommate if he gave her one more opportunity?

"Over here!" someone yelled.

"Help!"

"Don't block the exits."

Flames now leapt and roared from the back of the aircraft. The heat stung her back like a scalding acid. She wouldn't leave Willow. Some might say she was being heroic, but in truth she didn't think she possessed the energy to move. She was too tired to feel scared. The firefighters would save the two of them, or they wouldn't. Either way, time was running out.

"If there's anything you need to know right now," she whispered into her friend's ear, "it's how much God loves you."

"We've got the exits clear."

"I see someone there toward the back."

Kennedy wasn't ready to leave. There was more she was supposed to say. About sin and repentance, about Jesus' death and resurrection. Why was her brain so fuzzy?

"We're here. You're going to be ok."

Strong hands pried her to her feet.

"No!" She tried to kick but her legs collapsed beneath her. "No!" She thought she was screaming, but she couldn't hear herself.

"We'll send someone back to get your friend. But you've got to come with me now."

No. This wasn't how it was supposed to happen. She stretched her neck to look behind her, screaming at the flames that danced and flickered just a few feet away from Willow's body. No, this wasn't what was supposed to happen.

"Save her, not me." Kennedy was sobbing, but she didn't have the breath to make herself heard. Didn't have the energy to fight anymore. The faceless form of her anonymous rescuer held her in a steady, iron grasp as strong as the chains that clung to Ebenezer Scrooge's macabre partner.

"I have to go back," she whispered softly before her vision deserted her and everything fell to black, infinite darkness.

CHAPTER 20

Kennedy blinked her eyes open. Why did they hurt so bad? What was wrong with her contacts?

"Ow."

She tried to sit up.

Ow.

A man set his hand on her shoulder. "Easy there. Don't move too fast."

"Where am I?" Had she swallowed boiling water? Why did it feel like her lungs were burning?

Burning.

She threw his hand aside and sat up. The entire room spiraled in front of her. "Where is she?"

"Shhh." He put his finger to his lips like an over-doting nursery nanny. "You're at the hospital. Everything's going to be just fine."

"Where is she?" Kennedy asked again.

"The girl who was kidnapped? She's fine. She's in another room waiting for her dad to fly in and pick her up.

Everything's fine."

"No, it's not," Kennedy insisted. "Where's Willow?"

A nurse in Snoopy scrubs walked over. Whispered something to him. What were they saying? What was wrong with her roommate?

The nurse gave her a smile. As if she wanted to be on friendly terms. Kennedy wouldn't believe a word she said.

"You must have had an angel watching over you on that plane. You're a very lucky woman."

Kennedy didn't care about luck. Didn't care about who saved her or how or why.

The nurse lowered Kennedy onto her back. Why was she so weak? Why couldn't she stay seated on her own? She tried to swing her legs off the gurney. "I need to go."

"Not yet. You took in a lot of smoke back there."

She didn't care. She felt fine. If that's what you could call having your lungs covered in tiny pieces of ashy glass that cut you with every inhale.

"I need to find her."

The woman looked just as clinical when she was frowning as she had when she smiled. "I need you to stay still."

Kennedy pictured herself fighting her way out of bed. Exhaustion clung to each individual muscle fiber. Where was Willow? She turned her head. Why were the lights so bright? Patients were lined up on gurneys, and nurses scurried back and forth in front of a busy station. She didn't need to be here, wherever here was. She was fine. She didn't need all these gadgets and monitors. She turned the other way and looked out a small window but didn't recognize the parking lot outside.

Where was Willow?

Time passed with stubborn sluggishness. Nurses came in, went out. Hooked up an IV, smothered her face with an oxygen mask that made her feel like she'd suffocate from claustrophobia. She drifted to sleep. Woke up. Still no sign of Willow. Some of the other patients nearby were talking to official-looking businessmen with clipboards and recording devices. It would be Kennedy's turn any minute. If the other passengers were fine, so was she. If they were ready to give statements, so was she. Anything to get out of here.

Anything so she could find Willow.

"Excuse me, Miss. We found you with a backpack and an ID belonging to Kennedy Stern. Is that your name?"

Kennedy nodded at the professionally dressed woman with glossy black hair.

"I'm Michelle Boone with the Federal Air Marshall Service. Do you feel up to answering some questions about what happened on the flight? I've heard multiple reports now about a …"

"Is everyone ok?" Kennedy interrupted.

The woman frowned.

"On the plane," Kennedy pressed. "Did everyone get off safely?"

Agent Boone flipped a few pages on her clipboard. "Did you have a relative on the flight?"

"My roommate. We were traveling together."

An even deeper frown. "What is your roommate's name?"

"Willow Winters."

Something passed through the woman's eyes. Recognition. Compassion. Pity. She tapped her pen several times against the pages on her clipboard. "I'm afraid I'm not at liberty to discuss anyone's medical condition unless it's with immediate family. You don't …" She paused. Studied Kennedy. "You don't have a way to contact your roommate's next of kin, do you?"

Kennedy ripped the oxygen mask off her face and yanked the blood pressure cuff from her arm. She sat up, ignoring the dizziness that threatened to send her careening back into darkness.

"What happened to her?" She reached a hand back to

steady herself and stifled a cough that made a valiant effort to crush each one of her ribs.

Two medics scurried over, trying to coax Kennedy onto her back.

"Where's Willow?" she demanded. "Why won't you tell me what happened?"

The government agent held a hushed conversation with one of the medical professionals and finally turned back to Kennedy. "You need to lie down again, and then we can talk about your friend."

"Just tell me," Kennedy pleaded, but she allowed the nurses to lay her down. Tears leaked from her stinging eyes. Hot tears. Scorching tears. "Just tell me," she repeated and noticed that one of the women was holding her hand. What did she think that would accomplish?

Boone cleared her throat. "Your roommate was unconscious when we found her. She wasn't …"

Kennedy felt her throat muscles seizing shut. She wasn't hearing right. Something was wrong with her ears.

The agent swallowed once before continuing. "She wasn't breathing."

What was she saying? This was a government official. Why couldn't she answer one simple question?

"Where is she now?" Kennedy's voice was quiet.

Uncertain. Was she ready to hear the truth? Could she accept whatever news she received?

The Snoopy nurse was rubbing her back as if Kennedy were five years old and scared of the dark.

Boone's expression didn't change. "I haven't gotten an update yet, but I think it's probably wise if you ..."

The door to the makeshift triage unit swung open, and two paramedics pushed in a young woman sitting in a wheelchair. She was covered with several layers of blankets and twirled her blue hair around her finger. "All I'm saying is that if I'm gonna need a blood transfusion or anything, you need to guarantee it's coming from another vegan or I'm not accepting it."

Kennedy's body responded before her conscious mind figured out what was happening. She lunged out of bed, coughing in between peals of laughter, immediately tangling herself in the myriad wires that connected her to so many monitors and machines. "You're here!"

Willow fashioned a half-crooked grin. "Yeah, I'm all right."

Kennedy laughed until she choked on her own cough. "Where have you been?"

"Hypobaric chamber," Willow answered. "It was wicked awesome. You should try it."

"All right." A blond paramedic put his hand on Willow's shoulder. "I think that's enough excitement for now." He turned to Kennedy. "As soon as her oxygen levels improved she insisted on finding you."

Willow gave him a playful nudge. "You weren't supposed to say anything."

The federal agent tapped her clipboard. "Miss Stern, now that you've seen your friend's safe and sound, I really do need you to answer some questions for me. I have you listed as sitting in the back row by the lavatory. What can you tell me about a male passenger wearing Carhartts pants?"

CHAPTER 21

By the time the sun set through Kennedy's hospital room window, she had already spent two hours on her cell, first with her mom, trying to convince her she was alive and at least physically unharmed. Next she cried with Sandy while her pastor's wife convinced her that the emotional trauma of the day could lead to wholeness and healing with time and help from the Holy Spirit.

Kennedy had also walked the entire triage unit three times looking for Grandma Lucy, but none of the emergency responders recognized her description. She was exhausted after all her interviews with various federal officials. She was ready to leave Detroit behind, but the airlines as well as the hospital staff wanted her and Willow both to spend the night for observation. At least half of the passengers on Flight 219 had sustained injuries, some from smoke inhalation and some from the chaos that ensued when everyone tried to stampede off the plane at once.

By evening, though, the busyness and chaos at the

hospital died down, and Kennedy and Willow were wheeled on their gurneys into a room of their own. Kennedy's stomach flipped slightly when the nurses left and she was alone with Willow for the first time since their rescue. What was she supposed to do? What was she supposed to say? She'd made a promise with God, hadn't she? She couldn't just forget about it.

But how do you start a conversation like that?

"Wanna catch a flick?" Willow pointed the remote at the TV. "There's gotta be something interesting."

Kennedy didn't know what to say. Now more than ever she understood how quickly life can change. How quickly life can end. But she still couldn't bring herself to open her mouth and start a conversation she didn't think Willow was ready to have.

"Sure," she answered. "Just nothing too scary." She meant it, too. She was done with drama and terror. She'd even take one of her mom's cheesy farm romances if she had to. As Willow flipped through the channels, Kennedy shut her eyes, thankful when her body slipped off to sleep so her mind could finally enjoy some peace.

Her dad woke her up at six the next morning, ready to fire instructions over the phone in case any lawyers asked to talk to her. He was sure a suit against the airlines was inevitable and didn't want her to get taken advantage of by greedy attorneys. He also made her promise to call him before the airlines forced her to sign forms or waivers. Kennedy didn't care about any of that. She just wanted to forget the entire nightmare had ever happened. According to the most recent news reports, the only other passenger who died on the flight besides the murdered hostages was General himself. He was bound to a cabinet near the back lavatory and hadn't been able to free himself during the fire. His fat lieutenant in the Hawaiian shirt somehow escaped. At least they didn't recover any of his charred remains. Nobody knew what became of the passenger in Carhartts either, a man identified as an electrician with three kids who all attended Brown Elementary.

A nurse gave Kennedy discharge instructions right after her breakfast of stale English muffin and some sort of egg substitute, but she couldn't leave the hospital before passing another round of interviews with Michelle Boone and about half a dozen other Feds and airline workers. "They'll be here any time," the nurse told her cheerfully. By the time an orderly dropped off cold grilled-cheese sandwiches for lunch, the only person who had stopped in was the cleaning lady.

Kennedy and Willow passed the day playing Scrabble or watching corny sitcom reruns from their hospital beds.

Every time Kennedy thought she could muster up the courage to steer the conversation in a spiritual direction, she remembered how frightened she'd been on the plane and wanted to run away as fast as the little boy unfortunate enough to sing carols in front of Mr. Scrooge's office. She wanted to nap, but her body couldn't relax.

A liaison from the airlines knocked and entered their room at three thirty. It was seven at night before all the interviews were done and another airline employee handed Kennedy and Willow a hotel voucher and tickets to continue their trip to Anchorage the following morning.

"I can't believe we're stuck in Detroit another night," Willow complained. "How in the world are we supposed to get to this hotel?"

Kennedy didn't care how they traveled as long as they arrived without any further run-ins with terrorists.

Willow pulled her pockets inside out. "Seriously, how are we supposed to do anything? I don't have my wallet, I don't have my ID. How am I even going to get on the plane tomorrow?"

Kennedy's head was throbbing. "Let's just worry about that in the morning. They'll have records we were on that flight. It's not like they're going to keep us in Detroit forever."

As they walked through the hospital lobby toward the

exit, Julie Andrews crooned about bright copper kettles and warm woolen mittens. If Kennedy had the energy, she might have found the irony humorous.

"I'm dead serious, we need to go back and find that liaison lady. I can't do anything without my ID."

The last thing Kennedy wanted to do was backtrack. How could she explain how desperately she needed to get herself out of this hospital? She didn't care if they had to walk to the hotel as long as there was a bed waiting for her to collapse onto. In the past twenty-four hours since she arrived in Detroit, she doubted she'd slept three hours at any given stretch.

"I was wondering if I'd bump into you two again." The voice was too jocular. Too full of that raindrops-on-roses type of cheer that was so grating on her ears.

Kennedy stumbled ahead even as Willow stopped to give Ray the math teacher a half-convincing smile. "Hey, good to see you. Are you ok?"

He nodded. "Yeah, they discharged me earlier but I'm just now finishing all the interviews. You two? You both all right?"

No, Kennedy wasn't all right, and she wouldn't be until she found a bed to sink into. Preferably a bed with fluffed pillows and warm, heavy blankets.

"The airline gave me a hotel voucher." He checked inside an envelope he was holding. "The Golden Lion. You heard of it?"

"That's where we're going, too," Willow answered, and Kennedy wondered if she was going to give him their room number and a spare key as well.

"I don't know the bus system in Detroit. I think I'll just take a cab. You two ladies want to join me and split the fare?"

Willow fingered her glossy hair. "Actually, our wallets are incinerated by now, I'm sure."

"Well, I've got …" Kennedy began before Willow elbowed her in the ribs.

"Wow, that's rough. Then let me call a cab for all of us. It's the least I could do."

If Kennedy was lucky, it's all he would do.

Willow gave him a smile and positioned herself between him and Kennedy. "That would be fabulous." She linked her arm in his, and together they headed out into the freezing Detroit evening. By the time they arrived at the Golden Lion, Ray had invited both Kennedy and Willow to have dinner with him in the restaurant downstairs.

"My treat." He smiled at Willow, who had all but scrunched herself onto his lap on the cab drive over.

"I really need to get some rest." As soon as the words left Kennedy's mouth, she saw the grateful look on her roommate's face.

"Are you sure?" Ray asked. "You'll need to eat something eventually."

"I'm still feeling awful," she confessed. "I hardly slept at all last night. I just want to get to bed."

Before Willow followed Ray into the Golden Lion café, she leaned over and whispered in Kennedy's ear, "Don't worry about me if I'm late. I'll see you in the morning."

By the time her elevator took her to her room, Kennedy was too tired to care what Willow was doing or who she was doing it with. It was no different than life in their dorm room, really.

So much for telling her about the gospel, Kennedy mused as she plopped onto the bed. Her lungs still hurt whenever she tried to draw a deep breath. She thought maybe a hot, steamy shower would help clear out the last of the smoke and guck she'd inhaled, but she didn't think she had the stamina.

She shut the blinds to block out a dreary Detroit sunset, with more smog and clouds than actual sky. She thought about Alaska, about the northern lights she wouldn't be seeing. Not today, at least. She still wasn't even convinced she'd get on that plane and fly to Anchorage with Willow in the morning. Part of her was ready to swear off airplanes for good, take a bus back to Cambridge and spend Christmas with Pastor Carl and Sandy like she had last year.

As excited as she'd been for the big Alaska experience, she'd had enough adventure for one vacation already. She pulled out her phone and started searching Greyhound rates. If she caught a bus first thing in the morning, she could arrive in Boston by dinnertime. The Lindgrens wouldn't mind, and the Greyhound prices were reasonable. A hundred and five dollars for a one-way ticket. She could put it on her dad's debit card. Her parents were probably just as ready to have her grounded as she was.

It seemed like the most reasonable plan. Willow would understand.

She was struggling to decide if she'd rather leave at six in the morning or wait for the nine-thirty bus when her cell rang.

Dominic.

Her finger paused above the screen for just a moment before she answered. "Hello?"

"Hey, I'm so glad you picked up. I've been really worried."

"I'm sorry I didn't get hold of you sooner." Was it better

to confess she didn't have the energy to even think about calling him or cut off the apology there and leave it at that?

"No, don't feel bad. I'm just glad to hear you're ok. You're all right, aren't you?"

She didn't know if he was referring to her physical well-being or not. "Yeah, I'm fine." Maybe it was the fact that he had so much training in counseling that made it awkward to talk with him. She never wanted him to think that she was using him as a free shrink if she started discussing anything too deep.

"I saw some of the videos from the flight. That must have been really scary."

"It was." Could he tell she didn't want to talk about it?

"How's your roommate?" he asked. "Is she there with you?"

"No, she's out having dinner with some new fling."

"You sound upset." Why was he always so perceptive?

She plopped her head on the pillow and put him on speaker phone so she didn't have to hold the cell up to her ear. "I'm just tired."

"Are you mad that Willow's out enjoying herself after everything that happened?"

Sometimes she hated the way he could read her thoughts. "I don't know. It did seem kind of weird, I guess."

She could almost picture his patient smile on the other end of the line. "People react to stress in different ways."

"I know that." She'd taken AP psychology back in high school. She didn't need the lecture.

"But something else is bothering you."

She let out a sigh. Maybe by this time tomorrow she could breathe regularly without feeling like every exhale was a stifled cough. "I don't know. There was a minute ..." No, she wouldn't talk about the gunman holding Willow. That didn't matter. "After the fire started. She was stuck. There was a minute on the plane I didn't think she'd make it."

He didn't say anything. She could imagine the way he would study her if they were having this conversation face to face.

"And I felt guilty for not having shared the gospel with her beforehand," she finally confessed. It sounded so stupid now. As stupid as those people who try to make bargains with God when they're faced with their own mortality.

"So now you're upset that she's out on a date when you think she should be sitting with you asking you to tell her about the God who so miraculously saved her?"

She sighed again, wondering how annoying it would be to live with someone who could sense your emotions like some kind of a sci-fi empath. "I don't know. Something like that, I guess."

Another long silence. Something else she might never get used to.

"God works in people in different ways," he finally reminded her. "Don't give up on her. This is one night. You'll have a lot of free time together in Alaska."

"If I even go."

"What do you mean?"

She didn't want to spell out all her reasons. "I'm thinking of taking the bus home. Spend Christmas with Carl and Sandy."

"Well, I'm sure they'd love to have you. Just make sure you're not pulling a Jonah."

"A what?" Suddenly she wasn't as exhausted anymore. Maybe she'd find the energy for that steaming shower after all.

"God told Jonah to preach to Nineveh, and he ran away. It took a major crisis to get him back on the right track."

Dominic didn't know what he was talking about. The way he prattled on, he made it sound as if God sent the skyjackers to kill those people and set fire to the plane as a way to punish Kennedy for not preaching the gospel to Willow earlier. Kennedy had never been to seminary and certainly didn't know as much about theology as Dominic did, but she knew God would never act like that.

"Listen, I've got to go. My throat's really sore. It hurts to talk."

"I'd love to pray for you before you hang up," he offered.

"That's ok. I'd probably fall asleep right in the middle." She forced a laugh although she found the whole situation anything but humorous. She gave Dominic a *good night* that was slightly more abrupt than he deserved, and after a few minutes of internal debate, she pulled herself out of bed and started the shower running. Usually after a long flight, she couldn't wait to get out of her travel clothes. Wash off all the germs and grime from the air. Tonight, she couldn't even bring herself to undress. For one thing, when she got out of the shower she'd have to put on the same dirty clothes she had been wearing for the past two days, but there was something more to it than that. She couldn't stand the thought of her skin contacting the hot water. Couldn't stand remembering the way the heat from the flames had come so close to her and Willow before the rescue workers arrived. She sat on the toilet lid while the shower ran, but after a few minutes the heavy vapor reminded her too much of the smoke that had blinded her on the plane, and she shut off the faucet and opened the bathroom door.

She would never tell him to his face, but Dominic was right in just about every way. She was mad at Willow. She'd figured that this brush with death would finally make her receptive to the gospel, finally eager to hear the good news. Not to spend the night drowning her terror in booze, distracting herself and numbing her fears with a one-night stand.

She hated to admit it, but Dominic was probably right about the whole Jonah thing, too. If Kennedy took a bus back to Massachusetts, she wouldn't have to feel guilty that she wasn't telling Willow about Jesus' sacrifice on the cross. If she was five thousand miles and four time zones away from her roommate, nobody would expect Kennedy to share the gospel with her over Christmas break. She thought about Grandma Lucy, about her promise to pray for Willow. Kennedy had never gotten her phone number, had no way to contact her when and if that miracle ever happened. On the one hand, Kennedy was glad that Grandma Lucy had been on that flight to save Willow, but she resented the guilt that had glared down at her accusingly from the moment she met the old woman. Maybe Kennedy wasn't meant to be that outspoken of a believer. Was that any reason to make her feel so inadequate?

If God wanted Willow to be saved, if God wanted Kennedy to share the gospel with her, he would have to do all the work. He would have to direct the conversation the way it needed to go. He would have to give Kennedy the right words to say and Willow the open ears to hear. That was all there was to it. At first, Kennedy thought Willow's near-death experience would make her more receptive to spiritual matters, but if her behavior tonight was any indication, Willow planned to go on living her life as if Flight 219 never happened.

Well, God, looks like it's up to you.

Kennedy brushed her teeth with the hospital's cheap travel toothbrush and washed her face with their puny sliver of soap. It would probably be hours before Willow came back, if she returned tonight at all. Kennedy wasn't about to wait up for her. She had just made her way to bed when someone fidgeted with the lock outside. A little buzzer sounded, and the door swung open slowly.

"You asleep?" Willow's whisper flitted through the air like a mosquito.

"I'm here." Kennedy rolled over with a grumpy complaint that she stifled when she saw the soiled tears dribbling down Willow's face. "What's the matter?"

Willow shut the door behind her before letting out a suppressed sob.

Kennedy got out of bed tentatively. "Is everything ok? Did something happen with Ray?"

Willow shook her head and wiped her cheeks with the back of her hand. "It's not that." She sat down on the front of the bed, and Kennedy lowered herself beside her, feeling awkward and wondering what she should do with her hands.

"Are you upset about what happened on the flight?" she asked, recalling Dominic's reminder that people deal with shock and trauma in various ways.

"You're gonna think this sounds so stupid." Willow sniffed and tried to laugh at the same time.

"It won't be stupid," Kennedy assured her. "You know what a mess I can turn into. I'm the last person to judge."

Willow sniffed again noisily. "You promise you won't laugh?"

Kennedy had never seen her roommate so vulnerable before. Like a little child hoping her mother wouldn't yell.

"I promise."

"Something happened on that flight," Willow began, "and I've been trying to get it out of my head since I woke up in the hospital. But even over dinner with Ray, it was all I could think about. Out of everybody I know, I figure you're the only one who might be able to explain it to me."

"What is it?" Kennedy tried to keep her voice natural. If she'd learned anything during her times out with Dominic, it was how to be a more engaged listener.

Willow sighed and stared at her hands that fidgeted in her lap. "Ok, so I'm like most people I guess. I've always believed there was some sort of afterlife, heaven or whatever you want to call it. And like most people, I just assumed that if you do enough good with what life deals you, that's where you go when you die or whatever."

Kennedy nodded, afraid that if she tried to speak now she'd scare Willow away from finishing her thoughts.

"But then with the gun … and the fire …" Willow scratched at her arm as if all the painful memories were an itch she could brush off if she just scraped hard enough. "I started to think, *maybe I really am going to die*, and it scared the hell out of me. Literally. It probably sounds cliché to a church kid like you, but it scared me more than anything else. Thinking that maybe I hadn't been good enough. Maybe I didn't deserve to go to heaven. And how could I ever be sure? So I just thought that this flight might be a wake-up call for me, a chance for me to focus on the things that really matter so when my time does come, I'll be ready. But then I was sitting with Ray, and I mean, we all knew how the night was supposed to end and whatever, and at first I thought that'd be a great way for me to get past my fear and start living again, enjoying life. You know, like I always do. Things were going great, we were having fun together, but I realized there was no way I could relax with him, no way I could enjoy myself with him until I talked some of this stuff out."

She let out a little laugh. "I'm sure it sounds crazy. I mean, how can anyone be positive about heaven or hell or anything, you know? I really believe there's some sort of paradise waiting for people, but it's pretty arrogant to assume that you could ever know for sure if you've earned it, right?"

"It's not arrogant," Kennedy replied.

Willow frowned. "Well, maybe not for a church girl like you, but for someone like me ..."

"That's not what I'm saying. What I'm saying is you're right. Nobody can do enough good with their life to earn a spot in heaven. That's why we have to trust Jesus to make us worthy. And that's how we can be certain where we'll go when we die."

Willow raised one of her penciled eyebrows. "You really think there's a way to know for sure?"

"I do. I mean, think about Grandma Lucy on the flight."

"Who?"

"The old woman I was talking to earlier. The one who stood between you and the general when he had his ..." She stopped herself. "Don't you remember?"

Willow scowled. "The whole flight is such a blur right now."

Kennedy ignored the uncertainty that had started to heat up her gut and nodded. "Ok, well never mind her then. What I'm saying is that if you trust that Jesus has forgiven your sins, you're trusting that he's the one who can make you worthy of heaven. So it's not what you do, the good or bad or anything like that, it's what he did when he died on the cross for you."

The corner of Willow's mouth tilted up. "You should become a preacher. You sound so convincing."

Kennedy's whole core was trembling. She hoped Willow didn't notice. She knew that if she didn't ask the next question, there was no guarantee she'd find another chance like this again. "What about you?" she began awkwardly and cleared her throat. "I mean, is that something you want to learn more about, how to have your sins forgiven and stuff?"

Willow scrunched up her lustrous hair. "You've definitely gotten me curious, but there's no rush or anything. I mean, we'll have lots of time together at home to talk about whatever we feel like, right?"

Kennedy nodded her head as a gentle peace swept over her like silk sheets on a cool spring evening. "Right."

CHAPTER 22

"I'm so glad you talked me out of taking the bus back to Massachusetts," Kennedy gushed.

Dominic chuckled on the other line. "So you've enjoyed your time in Alaska so far?"

"It's insane. A lot of people out here don't even have their own water source. Willow's parents have to drive to the city well once or twice a week, fill up this huge tank, and dump the water into their storage room in the basement."

"And it doesn't freeze in the winter?" he asked. "Just how cold is it there?"

"When I woke up this morning, it was forty-eight below. Get this. Willow's dad took a pot of hot coffee, threw it up in the air, and it formed ice crystals and then completely evaporated before it hit the ground."

"Sounds like a great way to spend Christmas Eve. I'm really happy for you."

Kennedy stared out the window of Willow's room and watched the Winters' youngest goat leaping from one giant rock to another in his pen. It was only a little after three in the afternoon, but the sun was already setting.

"What about Willow? Have the two of you had any good discussions after everything that happened?"

Kennedy paced back and forth, studying all the paintings Willow had made back in high school. "It's been incredible. We've stayed up talking 'til one or two just about every night since I've been here. She says she's still not ready to become a Christian yet, but she has some great questions. When we get home, she's going to need a long talk with Pastor Carl or something, because most of them have me totally stumped."

"Oh yeah? Like what?"

Kennedy stared at the quilt Willow's grandma had sewn for her high school graduation. It was a winter scene with dazzling stars and the aurora borealis splashing bright greens and blues and yellows across the sky. "Ok, so for example last night she said one of the biggest reasons she hasn't become a Christian yet is she's afraid it would be intellectual suicide. She's really fixating on the whole evolution thing."

Dominic made a thoughtful sound. "Tell her lots of Christians believe in evolution."

"I know that, but I want her to..." What was she supposed to say next?

"You want her to believe the exact same way you do,"

Dominic finished softly. "It's ok. We all do that. It's just important to remember that it's Jesus who saves us, not theology."

"I know," Kennedy hurried to reply. "Oh, that reminds me of another good question she had."

"What's that?"

"So she wanted to know if she has to stop smoking weed before she gets saved."

"And you told her …?"

"I had no idea what to tell her," Kennedy confessed. "I mean, on the one hand, the Christian life's all about making sacrifices, denying yourself, right? But God doesn't expect us to be perfect in order to be saved or nobody would make their way into heaven at all."

"Sounds like you've got a lot to think about." There was a smile in Dominic's voice.

"Really? You're the one with the master's in theology and that's all you've got to say?"

"We can talk about it more when you're here. When do you fly back?"

"The thirtieth." Kennedy couldn't understand how her vacation had already sped by so quickly.

"Good. Because my cousin's throwing a New Year's Eve party, and I wanted to ask you to be my date."

"Your date?" Kennedy felt her face heat up. Why had she repeated the word like a mindless parrot?

"Yeah. I've been thinking about it ever since I heard about your flight on the news. I didn't want to bring it up the last time we talked because you were still so shaken up and everything, but thinking about you up there, knowing I was down here and couldn't do anything to protect you, it made me realize I'd been wanting to do this for a long time. So, now that I've completely embarrassed myself, will you come with me to my cousin's? It's part of our church group, actually. A chance to worship and pray in the New Year, ask God what areas in our lives he wants us to focus on, a real encouraging time."

Kennedy could think of better venues for a first official date, but then again, maybe this was part of God's plan for her all along. She could definitely tell her relationship with Christ was growing out here in Nowhere, Alaska. While Willow helped her mom with the barn chores, Kennedy usually hurried back inside as soon as her nose hairs froze. She'd been spending the extra time alone studying her Bible and praying. She couldn't remember another period in her life when she'd been so excited about her faith, so eager to see the kind of things God was doing around her. Willow was a perfect example. The fact that they could talk for two or three hours a night about salvation and not have it turn into one giant rant about the evils of organized religion was reason enough to believe in Christmas miracles.

Footsteps sounded on the stairs before Willow came in, her cheeks flushed with cold as she took off layer after layer of clothes and tossed them onto the bed. "Dinner's almost ready," she said. "Tell lover boy merry Christmas and hang up."

"I heard that," Dominic called out, and Kennedy turned her head so Willow wouldn't see how deeply she blushed.

"I gotta go," she told him. "The Winters have been working on this Christmas Eve dinner all day."

"Well, have fun. And if I don't get a chance to call you tomorrow, merry Christmas. I can't wait to see what blessings God has in store for us this coming year."

Willow was still staring, and Kennedy was still blushing, but she couldn't help it. "Yeah, me too," she replied lamely. "Merry Christmas."

"Merry Christmas, Kennedy."

Willow raised her eyebrow and smirked. From downstairs, Willow's dad called out, "Time for dinner, girls. Hurry up, Kennedy. I can't wait for you to try your first bite of Christmas moose."

CHAPTER 23

Kennedy had never seen a Christmas spread like the one that night at the Winters' table. Willow's dad had made moose meatballs with mushroom and asparagus gravy and a separate dish of halibut in a creamy sauce served on buttery pasta. He had çaught the halibut himself last summer, but the fate and demise of the moose were never mentioned at the table. The sides were as delicious as they were colorful: a green bean casserole with pine nuts, goat cheese, and stewed tomatoes; grilled cauliflower and Brussel sprouts; twice baked sweet potatoes whipped with cream and cinnamon; and a magnificent fruit salad with all kinds of produce Willow's dad had grabbed from an Anchorage fruit co-op before he picked up the girls from the airport.

"These are the best bread rolls I've ever eaten," Kennedy declared, smothering another spoonful of rosehip and fireweed jelly onto a golden-topped bun.

Mr. Winters sat up proudly in his chair. "Thanks. I mill the grains myself right before they bake."

"You should try the raspberry jam, too." Mrs. Winters passed the jar across the table. "We had a bumper crop this year."

After Kennedy was already past the point of full saturation, Mrs. Winters bent over the oven and pulled out dessert. "Here we have some strawberry rhubarb pie. Willow, did you get that whipped cream from the water room?"

Willow scooted back her chair. "No, I'll grab it now." She sprinted downstairs.

"The fridge was so full, we had to store a few things down there where it's cold," Mrs. Winters explained as she sliced through the flaky crust and heaped a generous portion on Kennedy's plate. "Now don't eat it yet. Wait for Willow. Have you ever had fresh whipped cream?"

"Not from a cow I've actually met," Kennedy answered.

Willow came up with a jar full of whipped cream and heaped two dollops on Kennedy's pie.

"Now eat it fast before it melts," Mr. Winters told her.

"No, that's the best part when it's all runny," Willow argued.

After dessert was tea, an herbal blend Mrs. Winters harvested and dried herself. "Do you like honey in yours?" she asked.

Kennedy nodded and held out her mug for a spoonful.

"Our bees did such a good job this year. Nothing like raw honey. Remind me, and I'll send some back with you to school. Great for allergies, you know."

Kennedy didn't think she had room for anything else in her stomach, but she'd been wrong. She sipped the tea slowly, enjoying the warmth and sweetness as it slid down her throat. "This is probably the most unique Christmas dinner I've ever had."

Mrs. Winters beamed at her across the table. "We're just glad you two girls are safe."

Kennedy stared at her plate. Some memories would spoil even the most abundant Christmas feast.

Willow's mom reached out and grabbed Kennedy's hand. "And we're glad our daughter's found such a good friend as you."

"That's right," her dad added. "Since her first day at Harvard last year, we've been hearing about you. How good you are with your studies, how respectful a roommate you are."

Kennedy glanced at Willow who shuffled uncomfortably in her seat. "Dad," she whined.

"What? When you have a good friend, it's important they know how you feel. It's not everybody who gets so lucky finding a best friend their first year of college."

"Dad," she repeated in the same tone.

"Ok. Ok." He raised his hands in surrender.

"But before we forget, we do have something for you." Mrs. Winters scooted her chair back. "To show you how much we appreciate your friendship with Willow." She passed Kennedy a small package wrapped in thick brown paper. "I found this at a craft bizarre I was selling at last month. The lady at the booth next to me had these beautiful handmade crosses, and I remembered Willow saying you're a Christian, and I thought you would love this."

Kennedy stared at the heavy crucifix in her hand.

"See the detail?" Mrs. Winters pointed to Jesus' brow. "See the thorns? It's so intricate. I hope you like it." She raised a questioning eyebrow.

"It's really nice," Kennedy stammered, "and very thoughtful." She'd never owned a crucifix before. Never even considered owning one, but she recognized the great amount of consideration that went into the present.

"She's not Catholic, Mom," Willow muttered.

"Well, how was I to know?" Mrs. Winters replied. "You said *Christian*. You didn't say anything else, so I just had to guess."

Mr. Winters cleared his throat. "We're a spiritual family, Kennedy," he explained, "and you probably already know this about us. We don't subscribe to one particular religion over any other, but we do consider ourselves people of faith. I was wondering if you had any Christmas traditions from your family or upbringing you'd like to share. It must be lonely with your parents doing their mission work all the way down in Africa ..."

"China," Willow corrected.

"China," her dad repeated, "so if you wanted, it would be an honor if you shared some of your family's traditions with us."

Kennedy wasn't ready to pull a Christmas Eve sermon out of her sleeve. She took another sip of tea. "Well, my dad always reads from Luke. That's the story of when Jesus was born. It starts with ..."

"Well, don't tell us," Willow's dad interrupted. "You say your dad reads it. So read it to us."

Willow stood up. "I'll go grab the Bible from upstairs. I know where it is."

Mr. and Mrs. Winters exchanged somewhat quizzical looks. While Kennedy waited for Willow to return, she stared around the Winters' dining room. A giant moose head hung on the wall, not what she expected as the décor for her vegan roommate's childhood home. Willow's grandmother had sewn several other arctic-themed quilts that were hung on the walls or draped over couches. In the far corner of the living room was a little library. On one side was a leather reclining chair next to a pile of fishing and hunting magazines and a shelf full of Greek classics. Right beside it was a rocking chair and a bookcase laden with *National Geographic*, *The New Yorker*, and literary fiction titles in pristine hardback. Kennedy tried to picture her roommate growing up as the only child out here in the middle of nowhere.

A minute later, Willow came downstairs with the Bible already open to Luke. Kennedy hadn't realized chapter two was so long. She decided to stick to the part about the shepherds, and as she read, she had to work past a lump in her throat. This was her second Christmas away from family. As kind and open-hearted as the Winters were, Kennedy missed home.

When she finished the passage, Willow's mom leaned back in her chair with a sigh. "I just love that part about the angels, all singing together. Do you believe there are angels here on earth?" she asked.

Kennedy tried to throw together some sort of a stammered reply.

"I suppose anything's possible, isn't it?" Mrs. Winters finally concluded.

Willow's dad leaned forward in his chair. "What next?" he asked.

Kennedy didn't understand what he meant.

"Is that all your family does? I mean, Jesus is the Savior of the whole world according to Christian tradition. I figured his followers would have a lot more to-do surrounding the day of his holy birth."

Kennedy glanced at Willow. Why hadn't she warned her to come to dinner prepared? "Well, we usually sing some songs."

Mrs. Winters clasped her hands together. "Beautiful! Would you like to use our piano?"

"I don't play," Kennedy hastened to explain. "I tried once, but ..."

"*A capella* it is then," Willow's dad declared with a thundering boom. "What should we start with? *Silent Night*?"

Kennedy's throat clenched shut for just a moment as she remembered her last Christmas in Yanji, as she and her parents and the refugees in their Secret Seminary sang *Silent Night* in Korean.

"Perfect." Mr. Winters breathed in deeply and started the carol for everyone.

As soon as they finished, Mrs. Winters jumped up from her chair. "Oh! What perfect timing. Take a look at this!" She scurried to the window as Willow's dad leapt from his seat, turned off the overhead lights and extinguished the candles on the table.

Kennedy was about to ask what was going on when Mrs. Winters threw back the curtains. The sky danced with streaks of green splashing from one end of the horizon to the other.

"Ooh!" Mrs. Winters pointed. "Look at that purple. I haven't seen it like that since Willow was little."

Kennedy stood mesmerized as the northern lights flickered from one end of the sky to the other. After the flashes of green came streaks of pink and violet, rippling like ribbons waved by dancers on a stage.

Kennedy felt a hymn of joy and praise rising from somewhere deep within her soul, a place that had been lying dormant until this very moment, a depth her mind had never accessed before.

She had never loved her singing voice, but she opened her mouth and let the words of praise flow from her. Willow and her family soon joined in, with her father taking a deep bass and her mother singing harmony in alto.

> *O holy night, the stars are brightly shining*
> *It is the night of our dear Savior's birth.*
> *Long lay the world in sin and error pining*
> *'Til he appeared and the soul felt its worth.*

When they reached the line about *a thrill of hope*, Kennedy glanced over at Willow, and in the light gleaming in from the glories outside, their eyes met. An understanding passed between them. The knowledge that they were now sharing Christmas not just as roommates, not just as friends, but as sisters, held together by bonds of fellowship stronger than any spiritual opposition or earthly terror.

The Winters were a little uncertain on the second verse, so Kennedy carried the melody along.

Chains shall he break for the slave is our brother

And in his name all oppression shall cease.

She didn't know what the future would hold. She didn't know what to expect in a week when she flew back to Boston and joined Dominic at his cousin's party. She didn't know what would happen in Willow's spirit or whether or not this new excitement in Kennedy's soul would withstand another busy semester of school.

All she knew was that right now, there was nowhere on earth she would rather be. Surrounded by a loving family, quirky as they were, and the glories of a majestic Creator who splashed his paints across the sky for everyone to see, Kennedy had never felt so thankful.

She had never felt so alive.

A NOTE FROM THE AUTHOR

I can't believe Kennedy is halfway through her sophomore year of college already! It feels like it's only been a few months since she was riding the T on her way to Carl and Sandy's new pregnancy center in *Unplanned*.

I want to say a big thank you to those of you who have made these Kennedy books so much fun to write. Your emails, questions, comments, and encouragement lift up my spirit in so many ways. I'm always happy to hear from you. You can contact me any time at alanaterry.com. It is a real joy getting to know so many folks from around the world!

My Kennedy books explore all kinds of hot-button topics (like police brutality, racism, abortion, and homosexuality). I like to keep her Christmas books a little lighter, with more suspense than heavy thematic issues. Even though I tried to give you a lighter novel than usual, I hope you were encouraged with Kennedy's growth as a Christian and

Willow's newfound interest in a relationship with Christ. For the record, I didn't write Kennedy to be a model believer. I wrote Kennedy to be a reflection. She has her faults, she has her blind spots. I truly believe that we can benefit when we read fiction about people as they really are, not as some omniscient author thinks they should be.

I'd like to thank Kaye and Mindy who are both nurses who helped me with the medical scene on the flight. Bill is a family friend, pastor, and EMS captain who fielded some questions about the emergency response at the airport. I'd also like to say a big thanks to Bart, a pilot who gave me a few tips about how he would handle a situation like the one Kennedy finds herself in. Josh is a civil engineer, and when I asked him for a good incentive to serve as the igniting point for the entire novel, he suggested I look into issues of environmental justice. I'm thankful for his advice as well as to Leslie L. McKee for her proof-reading skills.

Amy, I enjoy working with you as my editor so much. Jaime, you're the most rocking prayer partner and encourager ever! Here's also a shout out to my son who's taking over some of my computer and design jobs so I can spend more time working on Kennedy's next adventure instead of drowning in busywork. My prayer team, you are so awesome. I couldn't write these books without your intercession. Big thanks to my beta readers for your fabulous feedback, and a shout-out as well to my author friends who hold me accountable and make sure I'm making my daily writing goals.

My grandma died the week before I started drafting *Turbulence*, and I'd like to take this time to publicly express how thankful I am for her prayers and her legacy. I hope she would have liked seeing herself in Grandma Lucy.

I know for a fact I couldn't write a book without my husband's support and encouragement. I'd also like to thank the Lord who kept my body, mind, and computer running to bring you another Kennedy Stern Christian suspense novel!

DISCUSSION
QUESTIONS

For group discussion or personal reflection

If you're part of a book club and want to set up a skype meeting where I can meet with your group, let me know! You can contact me at www.alanaterry.com.

I always love to hear what readers think of my books. If you've read *Turbulence* and want to share your thoughts, I'm all ears!

Ice Breaker Questions

1. Do you like to travel? Why or why not?

2. What's the most memorable flight you've ever been on?

3. Would you rather spend your Christmas somewhere exotic or at home?

4. Who is the most interesting person you've met on an airplane, train, bus, etc.?

5. Who is a missionary whose life stands out to you as an example of Christian faith?

6. Who is the most courageous person you know?

7. What's the strangest food you've eaten at someone else's home?

8. Have you ever been to Alaska? Would you like to go?

Story-Related Questions

1. How did *Turbulence* compare to any of the other Kennedy Stern books you've read?

2. What did you find to be the most exciting or suspenseful part of the story?

3. What do you think about Grandma Lucy's character? Do you know anyone like her?

4. What would you have done if you were a passenger on Flight 219 with Kennedy and Willow?

5. Do you think Kennedy should feel guilty for not witnessing to Willow sooner?

6. What do you expect will happen in future Kennedy books? Are there any themes or issues you'd like to see her explore in depth?

Issue-Based Questions

1. Are you afraid of flying? Did 9/11 change your ideas of travelling by air?

2. Have you ever shared the gospel with a friend even though you were scared to?

3. Do you think it's easier to share the gospel with your friends and family or people you don't know very well?

4. If you went through something like Kennedy did on Flight 219, do you think you'd be bolder in the future about sharing your faith?

5. Did you feel sympathetic for the issue General brought up about the elementary school? Have you heard of issues like this in real life?

Books by Alana Terry

North Korea Christian Suspense Novels

The Beloved Daughter

Slave Again

Torn Asunder

Flower Swallow

Kennedy Stern Christian Suspense Series

Unplanned

Paralyzed

Policed

Straightened

Turbulence

Infected

See a full list at www.alanaterry.com

Made in the USA
Middletown, DE
22 May 2022